THE
MIDNIGHT
LIBRARY

—

SHUT YOUR MOUTH

DAMIEN GRAVES

SCHOLASTIC INC.

New York   Toronto   London   Auckland   Sydney
Mexico City   New Delhi   Hong Kong   Buenos Aires

SPECIAL THANKS TO
SALLY JONES AND ALLAN FREWIN JONES

—

ISBN-13: 978-0-439-89393-0
ISBN-10: 0-439-89393-3

Series created by Working Partners Ltd.
Text copyright © 2006 by Working Partners Ltd.
Interior illustrations copyright © 2006 by David McDougall

12 11 10 9 8 7 6 5 4 3 2   8 9 10 11 12/0

Printed in the U.S.A.
First printing, August 2007

Welcome, reader.

My name is Damien Graves,
curator of that secret
institution:

The Midnight Library.

Where is The Midnight Library, you ask?
Why have you never heard of it?
For the sake of your own safety, these questions are better left
unanswered. However . . . as long as you promise not to reveal
where you heard the following (no matter who or *what*
demands it of you), I will reveal what I
keep here in my ancient vaults.
After many years of searching,
I have gathered the most terrifying
collection of stories known to
humanity. They will chill you to
your very core, and make
the flesh creep on your young,
brittle bones. So go ahead, brave
soul. Turn the page. After all, what's
the worst that could happen . . . ?

Damien Graves

LOOKING FOR DAYLIGHT? KEEP DREAMING.
THE MIDNIGHT LIBRARY CONTINUES....

—

VOICES

BLOOD AND SAND

END GAME

THE CAT LADY

LIAR

SHUT YOUR MOUTH

I CAN SEE YOU

THE CATCH

THE
MIDNIGHT LIBRARY:
VOLUME VI

Stories by Sally Jones and Allan Frewin Jones

——

CONTENTS

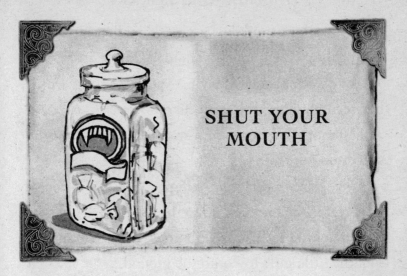

SHUT YOUR MOUTH

Hey, you! *What are you doing?*"

Louise nearly leaped out of her skin. Niki, Laura, and Sarah had crept up behind her as she sat waiting for them in the park. She'd been talking to a little kid who was giving her toy rabbit a ride on the swings, and Niki had bellowed right into her ear. Niki, Laura, and Sarah doubled over, laughing and pointing.

"Very funny — not," Louise muttered, trying to keep her cool. From where she was sitting, it seemed as though Niki towered over her, red hair fizzing out from her head like a fiery halo. Louise knew that Niki

1

could be a lot of fun, but it was normally only if you went along with what *she* wanted to do.

"Your face!" Laura was saying, spitting out the words between giggles. "You went, like . . . *oooh . . . wuh . . .*" And she opened her mouth in a big *O*, flashing the braces on her teeth.

"Hey, you — off the swing!" Niki said. Louise watched as she marched up to the little girl. "And take your stupid fluffy rabbit with you!" she finished, batting the little girl's toy onto the ground.

Louise hated it when Niki got like this. "Just leave the kid alone, Niki —" she began, but Laura interrupted her. "Didn't you see the sign?" Laura chimed in. "NO ANIMALS ALLOWED!"

"But . . . it's not a real animal," the little girl murmured. Louise could see that the girl was intimidated by the others. Her face had drained of color, and she kept looking up quickly, and then returning her gaze to the floor.

"Sorry, it still counts as an animal if it's got four legs and a tail," Sarah said, pretending to look very serious.

"Hey, girls, let's leave her alone. She's not hurting

anybody," Louise said, trying to distract Niki and the others.

"Just get off the swing, kid, and disappear," Niki said, ignoring Louise completely.

At that moment, Louise saw a woman walking over toward the swings at a brisk pace. *Thank goodness — this must be the kid's mom*, Louise thought. *She'll put Niki in her place.* As the woman approached, Niki leaned down close to the little girl.

"Don't even think about blabbing to your mom!" Niki hissed. The girl pulled away as though she'd been stung and ran off.

"Looks like she's just seen the wicked witch!" Sarah giggled.

"She has!" Niki replied, grabbing the swing. Laura and Sarah joined Niki but Louise hesitated. *This is so boring*, she thought. *I remember when you three were fun, but that was before you turned into such bullies.* Then she noticed that Niki was giving her one of her weird looks. Louise knew the look well. It meant, *Are you with us or not?*

"What?" she said, staring back at Niki.

"You can be *so* touchy sometimes," Niki said, and Louise felt her face redden as Laura and Sarah frowned at her.

Louise opened her mouth to say something, then shut it again. It was no good. If she tried to explain herself, she'd only make it worse. "I'm just a little stressed about that math test we had, that's all," she lied. Forcing a smile, she grabbed a swing and joined in.

"Girls — over there," said Sarah. "Looks like we've got trouble." Louise watched the girl's mother go marching up to an attendant and point toward the four of them. *Oh, no,* Louise thought. *Nice one, Niki — she'll want our names, and then what school we go to, and all for these stupid swings that we're too old for anyway.*

Niki jumped off. "We're out of here! That little blab-bermouth has told on us."

The attendant was gesturing at them, and he broke into a run. Louise slowed the swing with her feet, got off, and bolted toward the park gates along with the other three. The attendant gave chase, and Niki, Laura, and Sarah began to hoot with laughter. Louise couldn't help laughing, too, as she saw the attendant, who was a heavy-set, red-faced man with short legs, trying to catch them.

"You girls! Stop right there!" he puffed.

"It's like being chased by a beach ball!" Laura panted.

As they reached the gates, Louise glanced back to see that the attendant had given up. Laura and Sarah flopped down on a bench. Louise felt relieved that they weren't going to get caught this time. However, that feeling of relief evaporated when Louise saw the little girl from the swings. The girl was sobbing and clutching her mom's legs.

"Well, girls," said Niki. "That brat has just ruined our afternoon's entertainment. Who's next on our hit list?" she said, a broad grin stretching across her face.

Louise knew what was coming.

"Mr. W-W-Webster!" Sarah said.

"My thoughts exactly!" said Niki, smiling.

Mr. Webster owned the quaint old candy shop in the little row of stores opposite the park. Louise thought that Webster's Delicious Delights was the most amazing shop she had ever been in. Mr. Webster made all the candy himself in the kitchen at the back of the store. Each one was totally unique and tasted so much better than the mass-produced stuff.

"OK!" Niki said as they reached the shop. "What's on the menu today?"

"I don't believe it," Sarah moaned. "I've only got a few dimes left!"

"Don't worry about it," Niki said, smiling the smile that Louise had grown to distrust. "Who needs money?"

"What are you suggesting?" Laura asked with a laugh.

"Well, he shouldn't charge so much, should he?" Niki said bitterly.

Louise hated it when her friends got like this. She had known the girls since they were all small, and she knew that none of them *needed* to take anything from stores without paying. But for some reason, Niki had started doing it recently, and Laura and Sarah soon joined in. Louise wasn't sure about the person that Niki was turning into. "I've got some cash, so I'm going to pay for mine anyway," she said, trying to make it sound casual.

Niki scowled at her. "You're no fun, Louise. Why don't you just go home?" There was a vicious edge to her voice.

Louise swallowed hard. She could hear her heart pounding in her ears. "I'll go where I want, when I want. You're not my mom, Niki, so just back off." Louise could feel Laura and Sarah staring at her in disbelief, but she refused to let her gaze waver, looking steadily at Niki.

There was a long pause, then, suddenly, Niki flashed a big grin. "That's my girl," she said, slapping Louise on the back. "I can always count on you to play along with my jokes!"

How was that a joke? Louise wondered angrily. Niki banged through the door, making the bell jangle loudly. Louise tried to calm herself down. *I don't have to do anything I don't want to*, she told herself firmly.

Entering the cool interior of Webster's always felt like traveling back in time. The smell of chocolate mixed with the aroma of polish on the ancient wooden counters, and it was like nothing else Louise had ever known. She loved the way the colored windowpanes made the light in the store seem dim and mysterious.

The rainbow colors flickered over the shelves with their rows of huge glass jars, full of amazing candies of every size and shape. They seemed to glow like jewels.

"HEY, MR. WEBSTER! WE'RE HERE!" Niki shouted, shattering the calm inside the shop.

Louise followed Niki, Sarah, and Laura over to the curving mahogany counter that took up one side of the store. She inspected the glass-fronted display of chocolates and other candies, some so special they were individually wrapped and priced.

Mr. Webster came shuffling out from the back room in his shabby old slippers. He had a bald head that looked like he polished it, pink speckled cheeks, and small eyes that peered at them over his ancient-looking spectacles.

"I knew it was you girls," he grumbled. "You're like a herd of wild elephants." He stood waiting for them to order, and Louise could feel tension rising inside her as she watched Sarah switch around the signs on the displays, right in front of the storekeeper.

"W-w-what d'you think you're doing?" Mr. Webster spluttered. Louise knew that when Mr. Webster got upset or angry, he started to stutter. She felt sorry for him because Niki, Laura, and Sarah only seemed to act meaner whenever it started happening.

"Just trying to help you, Mr. Webster," Sarah replied, wearing an innocent look. "I think this one goes here, doesn't it?" She picked up a sign saying MANGO SURPRISE and replaced it with one saying BANANA RIPPLE.

"Leave that alone!" Mr. Webster made a grab for the sign. But before he could reach it, Sarah handed it to Laura.

"Come on, Mr. Webster," Laura said, moving out of his reach. "Surely, you know it's rude to grab."

Louise watched as Niki leaned over a nearby DO NOT TOUCH sign. She was cramming chocolate into her mouth, appearing not to care whether Mr. Webster was watching or not. Louise felt a knot of anxiety coiling in her stomach. They really seemed to have it in for Mr. Webster.

"Now where can we put this?" Laura said, moving the sign over to the other side of the store.

But Mr. Webster had spotted Niki. "Anything y-y-you touch, you'll pay f-for," he said angrily.

"Pay for what? I haven't touched anything!" Niki

replied. "Prove it, Webster," she said, flashing him a defiant look.

"You saw her, didn't you?" Mr. Webster spun around and faced Louise. "I bet you've been taking things, too."

"I haven't. Honestly!" Louise replied indignantly.

"C-c-can't you read?" Mr. Webster said, sweeping past her, heading for Laura. "It says DO NOT TOUCH."

"Oh, no, I thought it said DO TOUCH! Silly me. You really should write your signs better, Mr. Webster," Laura replied.

"B-b-b —" Mr. Webster began.

Louise found herself smiling in spite of herself. It was quite a funny sight, with Mr. Webster rushing around trying to stop Niki, Laura, and Sarah from rearranging his carefully constructed displays.

At that moment, Louise felt something pulling at her side. Looking down, she saw that Niki had stuffed a large handful of foil-wrapped treats into Louise's jacket pocket. Louise tried to shove them down farther, so they were out of sight.

"What are you doing?" she hissed at Niki. She could feel her cheeks burning.

"Shh! Keep quiet or else we'll get caught," replied Niki, spitting the words back at Louise.

Louise was mortified. If she got caught, there was no way she could explain this without either looking like a dork in front of the girls — or like a thief in front of Mr. Webster. She hated Niki for putting her in this situation. Louise concentrated as hard as she could. *Don't blush — he'll know you've done something wrong*, she ordered herself.

"So are you buying anything, or not?" Mr. Webster demanded, staring hard at Louise. She felt Niki nudge her in her side.

"Hmm . . . I'm not sure. What do you think, Louise?" Niki said, staring at Louise and smiling a horribly smug smile.

"Nothing today," she said quickly. "I was . . . just checking that no one had taken my cell phone," she said, patting her pocket.

"Hey, girls, look at those!" Niki said. She was staring at the top shelf. A small stack of red velvet-covered boxes had been placed there. Shining satin ribbons trailed from the boxes and curled down over the shelf.

And printed in gold lettering on the edges of the boxes were the words WEBSTER'S SPECIALS. The boxes looked more beautiful than anything Louise had ever seen in the store.

"What's in those, Mr. Webster?" Louise asked.

Mr. Webster pushed his glasses higher up on his nose. "None of your business."

"But can't we buy some?" asked Niki.

"Absolutely not," Mr. Webster snapped. "They're new, and they're not for you."

"Why not?" Sarah replied hotly.

"Forget it, Sarah." Niki turned back to Mr. Webster. "Keep your stupid old boxes," she jeered. "They wouldn't be special enough for us, anyway. Come on, girls." Laura and Sarah followed her out of the store. Louise took one more look at the velvet boxes before going out, too.

That candy must taste *really* good if it's in boxes like that," Sarah said as they trudged down the street. Louise was hardly listening. She was thinking about what Niki had done in the store. She thrust her hand into her pocket and pushed the stolen candy into Niki's chest.

"Don't you *ever* do that to me again!" she said. "If you want to take things, do your own dirty work."

Niki looked shocked for a second. "*Oooooo . . .*" she smiled. "Touchy!"

"Yeah! Stop scaring us, Louise!" Laura teased.

"Don't worry, LouLou," said Niki. "I always do my own dirty work." She pulled out handfuls of candy from her own pockets. "I just thought you might like to live on the wild side for once. Guess I was wrong!" she said, rolling her eyes.

It was Friday, and the girls were having a sleepover at Sarah's house. Sarah had rented their favorite movie, and her mom had made some delicious chili con carne. Louise was having a really good time — just four friends laughing about the stupid stuff that goes on at school.

The movie was coming to the scene where the girls usually recited all the lines. It involved a lot of romantic dialogue and intense emotions.

But something was wrong. Louise looked at Niki, who pushed aside her bag of microwave popcorn with a look of disgust. "This tastes like cardboard," she grunted.

Louise could feel the mood in the room change. Laura quickly looked across at Sarah and switched off the TV without a word.

"Why wouldn't he sell us that candy?" Niki said quietly, pretty much to herself. "They must be *really* exclusive," she breathed. "That's why he keeps them out of reach."

"Maybe he uses the best cocoa beans for the chocolate," Laura suggested.

"And all the other ingredients come from a top-secret factory," Sarah said in hushed, dramatic tones.

"Whatever makes them special is going to stay a secret, anyway," said Louise. "Those boxes are way too high up for us to reach."

"Well . . . if he's not *selling* them," Niki said with a big grin, "we'll have to help ourselves."

"Yesss!" hissed Sarah.

"But how can we get them? They're on the top shelf," Louise said. She hoped the problem of them being so high up would prevent Niki from planning anything.

"We'll have to wait until there aren't any customers," Niki said. "Then find some way of getting Mr. Webster out the back."

"That's not going to be easy," Louise pointed out desperately. She wanted to nip this plan in the bud now, so that Niki would move on to some other idea.

Niki stopped for a second. "Maybe we could tell him we smell something burning in his kitchen —"

Laura interrupted her. "No, what we do is call Mr. Webster. I've never seen a telephone in his store, so I'm betting that it must be in the kitchen."

"Then what? The rest of us sneak in and take the boxes?" Louise watched as Sarah put two and two together in her head.

"You've got it," Laura replied.

"Sounds good to me," Niki said. Then she turned to Louise. "You in?"

Louise thought for a moment. *It's only some stupid candy. It's not like anyone will get hurt in the process. And I'm never going to hear the end of it if I don't.*

15

"Well?" Niki asked.

Louise took a deep breath. "I'm in," she said.

Louise and the others stood in the entrance to the park, watching the shoppers wandering down the street.

"OK," Niki said, her gaze fixed on Webster's store window. "Who's going to make the phone call?" She turned to look pointedly at Louise. Louise prepared herself to say no, because she was sure that she'd be far too nervous to be a convincing customer.

"Wait — Laura! You're good at voices," Niki said suddenly, and Louise felt instant relief. No way did she want to have to make a prank call.

"Cool!" Laura looked really enthused. "OK. Here goes. This is the trial run. 'Well, hello. Is this Mr. Webster? Great. I'd simply love —'"

"Don't go over the top!" Niki hissed at her angrily.

Laura shifted uncomfortably under Niki's glare. "All right, Niki — sheesh. 'Anyway . . . so if you'd just gather a few items for me, that would be marvelous. I'd like them put into gift boxes and wrapped in some gold paper. You do *have* gold paper —'"

Niki stopped her, mid-flow. "OK — good enough."

Louise suddenly had a thought. "What happens when nobody turns up to pick up the order?"

Niki let out an overly dramatic sigh. "Chill *out*, Louise. By the time the old man realizes what is going on, we'll have gotten a couple of those special boxes."

"Where should we hide beforehand?" Louise asked, scanning the opposite sidewalk.

"What about behind those?" Sarah pointed at a row of mailboxes.

"People might see us and wonder what we're doing," Louise replied.

"Live dangerously for once, Louise!" Niki grinned, shoving her in the arm. Before Louise could respond, Niki ran off toward the store, barely looking before running across the busy street. Sarah followed her a second later, and Louise found that she, too, was moving faster and faster. She could feel excitement taking the place of nerves and followed Sarah's lead, barely paying attention to the drivers honking their horns around them. With the blood rushing in her ears, she made it across the two lanes of traffic. A van screamed to a halt right next to her, and the driver hooted furiously and rolled down his window. "Look where you're going!" he yelled.

"Sorry!" Louise grinned, and looked up to make sure that Mr. Webster hadn't seen the commotion, before joining Niki and Sarah behind the mailboxes.

Niki was fuming. "What are you *doing*? You could have blown the whole thing!"

"Bet old Webster saw you." Sarah tucked a stray blonde curl back under her wool hat, looking furious. "He'll be watching out for us now."

Through the old, colored windowpanes, Louise could just make out Mr. Webster serving a customer. She crouched down beside Niki and Sarah. "It's OK. He's with a customer. There's no way he saw me," she said.

"This is just like being in a movie," Sarah said.

"I hope it's not *Mission: Impossible!*" Louise whispered back.

"OK, so this is what we're going to do: When Webster goes out back to answer Laura's call, we get in there and find something to stand on. Then we get a couple of the special boxes, and get out," Niki instructed. "Louise, while Sarah and I get the boxes, you lean against the kitchen door to prevent Webster from coming out."

Now all we do is wait for the customer to leave, thought Louise. She could feel a strange mix of excitement and gut-turning anxiety coursing through her body.

"Please don't let anyone else go in," prayed Sarah.

"Come on. Get out of the store," Niki said under her breath.

The couple of minutes they waited for the last customer to leave the store felt like an hour. The woman walked past the girls carrying a large, gold-wrapped package. Louise, Niki, and Sarah did their best to look inconspicuous. Louise stared pointedly at the ground, and Sarah decided to concentrate on her text message in-box.

After a moment, Niki spoke up. "Get ready! This is it! Double-check that she was the last one in, then we can get going." Louise got up and casually walked past the window. She caught a glimpse of Mr. Webster putting a jar back on a shelf. He had his back to her, so she slowed down, making sure that he was really on his own.

"All clear," she whispered to Niki and Sarah.

Niki signaled to Laura, who was standing ready by the park gates. Louise stayed put on the other side of the store, just out of view from the inside, and waited for Laura to make the phone call. Sure enough, a telephone rang in the back of Mr. Webster's shop, and Louise watched as he hurried out the back, closing the door behind him.

"Go!" Niki said, her eyes glinting.

Louise walked over and opened the door, and Niki and Sarah quickly entered. They could hear Mr. Webster's muffled voice talking on the phone, and Louise could just make out a few snippets of his conversation.

". . . of course . . . no trouble at all. Just a moment, I'll get a pencil . . . No, that's wonderful, wonderful . . ."

"Get something to stand on," Niki whispered to Sarah.

"There! Under the counter." Sarah had spotted a stool that looked just about tall enough. Louise watched, her heart pounding in her chest, as Niki and Sarah gently lifted the heavy wooden stool and set it down near the old-fashioned shelves where the special boxes were stacked.

"Louise, go and see what's going on with Webster," Niki said as she carefully climbed onto the old wooden stool. Louise walked over and leaned close to the large door that led through to the kitchen. She tried to calm her breathing in case Mr. Webster heard.

"So let me get it straight, Miss. You'd like thirteen boxes of the . . ."

Louise turned back to Sarah and Niki and gave them a thumbs-up. Niki grinned at her and managed to haul herself upright on top of the high stool. Sarah stood underneath her, holding her as securely as she could. Louise was glad that it wasn't her up on that stool. It looked a little too unstable.

Suddenly, Louise heard Mr. Webster raise his voice.

"This is all a joke to you, isn't it, young lady?" He was shouting. She'd never heard him this angry before. "Well, it *isn't* to me. This is my livelihood. I'll find out who you are, don't worry. And then you'll be sorry —"

"He's onto Laura!" Louise hissed to Niki and Sarah. "Quick — I'll try to hold the door, but we have to go *now*."

Niki stared at her, frozen, fingertips touching the special velvet boxes.

"Hurry!" Louise said urgently as she leaned against the door as much as she could.

Suddenly, the kitchen door began to rattle.

"Who's out there?" Mr. Webster shouted. "You'll be sorry! You'd better hope I don't get hold of you."

Louise's excitement was swept away by a torrent of fear and regret. As she jammed her foot at the base of the door, a wave of panic rose within her. *What had she been thinking?* She knew that this was a thoroughly stupid plan, and she felt hot with anger for allowing herself to go along with it.

The door shook alarmingly. Mr. Webster must be throwing his weight against it.

"Niki! I can't hold on! He's —"

At that moment, Louise felt herself being flung away from the door. She landed heavily on one knee and felt it twist under her weight. The pain was bad, but she immediately forgot it as Mr. Webster burst through, looking around wildly. The look in his pale eyes sent a chill right through her.

"What on earth's going on?" he raged. There was no sign of his stutter anymore. "You'll pay for this!" he screamed. As he came toward them, Louise felt terrified.

Everything that followed seemed to happen in slow motion. Niki, fingers clutching at one of the special boxes, lost her balance. Louise watched as the stool tilted and Niki began to fall. In an attempt to save herself, Niki grabbed at a shelf holding several large glass jars. Her weight tore the entire thing from the wall. The jars came crashing down, and Louise shielded herself as glass exploded and gumballs scattered everywhere. Mr. Webster seemed so stunned that he was rooted to the spot. There was a second's terrible silence as they all stared, round-eyed, at the destruction around their feet.

"RUN!" shouted Niki.

Louise felt as if someone had pressed a switch inside her. She felt her muscles explode with energy as she headed for the door, desperate to escape. Niki's shout seemed to be the signal for Mr. Webster to spring to life, too. He was purple with rage, moving faster than she would have ever thought possible.

"Niki, watch out!" Louise shouted.

"Got you, you little vandal!" Mr. Webster said triumphantly as he grabbed Niki by the upper arm and dragged her around to face him.

"Let *go* of me!" Niki screamed. "Aargh, get off! That hurts!"

"Why have you done this?" Mr. Webster said, shaking her furiously. "Look at the mess. All my work. Ruined!"

Niki looked terrified. Louise was suddenly very worried about what Mr. Webster might be capable of doing. She charged at the storekeeper, knocking into his side. In the confusion, Niki managed to free herself and dived under his arm, kicking out at his ankle as she did. Caught off balance, Mr. Webster stumbled and crashed onto the floor. Seizing the moment, heart pounding madly, Louise went racing after Niki, feet crunching in the spilled wreckage as she reached for the door.

Laura was waiting as Niki and Louise came rushing up, and the three of them almost fell through the park gates and into the shrubbery. Louise sat down heavily on the grass, relief washing over her.

"I'll never go near that store again," Niki said, pulling

up her sleeve to reveal a hand mark. "He grabbed me so hard. It really hurt!"

"But what's happened to Sarah?" Laura asked. "Where is she?"

Louise and Niki looked at each other.

"She must have been caught," Louise said, the small feeling of relief disappearing again immediately.

Niki glared at Louise. "You blew it! It's your fault he's got Sarah."

A fit of rage consumed Louise. "My fault? It was your stupid plan. That's why Sarah got caught, and it's thanks to me that you didn't get caught, too!"

Niki seemed to shrink. After a moment, she broke the silence, staring at the red marks on her arm. "What an idiot!" she grumbled. "Look what he's done!"

Louise didn't bother to reply. She scanned the street, half hoping that Sarah had made it out of the store and that she'd chosen to go home or maybe around the block.

"I'm going to report him," Niki said, scowling. "You can almost see his fingerprints on my arm. It's against the law to grab somebody like that!"

Something in Louise suddenly snapped. "Oh, right! So who *exactly* are you going to report him to?"

Niki looked up in surprise. "What?"

"Were you thinking of telling the police?" Louise asked pointedly.

"No . . . I was just . . ." Niki said with a frown.

Louise could feel her voice becoming strong and forceful. "'Cause they'd be really interested, wouldn't they?" Louise went on. "Hmmm . . . let's see. What would you say? 'We were trying to steal stuff, and the owner of the store tried to stop us.'" She smiled grimly. "Oh, yeah, Mr. Webster would be in real trouble. Yeah, right!"

Sullenly, Niki pulled down her sleeve.

"It's OK for you," she muttered. "He didn't grab you. But he seems to have grabbed Sarah. She's still in there."

Niki looked away.

"We have to go back for her," Louise said. "We have to say we're sorry to Mr. Webster."

"Sorry? No way!" Niki said, shocked. "Are you crazy?"

"We might get off easier if we do. This was a stupid plan from the start," Louise said, staring hard at Niki.

Niki looked furious. "Oh, right! So if it was so dumb, why didn't you say you didn't want to do it?"

Louise was silent for a second. Why *hadn't* she? There'd been so many times when she'd wanted to say what she thought. But each time, she'd chickened out, afraid she wouldn't be one of the group anymore.

There was a moment's uncomfortable silence, only punctuated by the noise of cars and motorcycles rushing by on the nearby street.

Suddenly, Laura piped up. "Louise is right," she said to Niki. "We can't leave Sarah. We have to go back."

Niki looked shocked. Louise thought it was probably the first time Laura had ever disagreed with her.

"Well, you can do whatever," Niki grumbled. As she spoke, she pulled something out from under her jacket. The other two stared. It was a red velvet box with curling satin ribbons and gold letters on the side.

"Oh, wow! Awesome!" Laura said enthusiastically.

Louise stared in disappointment at the pieces of candy inside the box. They looked like the most boring edibles in the world — the same size and shape and color as Ping-Pong balls.

"What's so special about those?" Niki said, taking one out and turning it over.

"What a rip-off!" Laura said. "Stupid old Webster must have tricked us!"

Louise frowned. "It's weird, isn't it? They just look like huge gumballs."

"Maybe they *look* boring, but inside they're amazing," Laura said hopefully.

Louise, Niki, and Laura each took one of the special candies and began to suck on it. Louise felt like spitting it out. The gumballs were as nasty-tasting as they were boring-looking.

"It tastes like paper," Laura said with her mouth full.

"Paper would have been less of a hassle to get!" Niki said grimly.

Louise crunched down on hers, and it shattered in her mouth. After a moment's chewing, she said, "We'd better go back to the store and find Sarah." She swallowed hard, and the fragments of the candy were gone.

"OK," Niki said, sighing. Laura gave a little nod as if she didn't trust herself to speak.

As they began to make their way toward Mr. Webster's store, Louise swallowed again. The candy had left a faint, coppery tang in her mouth.

The three girls waited for the traffic lights to change so they could cross the street. They were in no hurry this time. Mr. Webster's shop now looked quite different to Louise — not inviting or exciting at all. As they crossed, Louise noticed that the old beige blinds had been drawn across the window so you couldn't see in.

She was beginning to feel very shaky. Her entire face felt like it was a little sunburned, and at the same time her hands, feet, and neck tingled as though she'd been lying in the snow. She definitely wasn't looking forward to seeing Mr. Webster again.

They arrived at the store. The sign now read CLOSED, but the door was still slightly ajar. Louise turned to Niki and Laura. "Ready?" she asked.

The other two nodded, not looking ready at all. Louise opened the door and stepped into the store. In the gloom, she could see Mr. Webster, stooped down, slowly brushing the mess into a pile in the corner of the shop. As they entered the store, he looked up, and Louise braced herself for him to start shouting again.

But his expression didn't change. He stared at them for what felt like ages, and then, wordlessly, began to clean up again. There was no surprise in his face at all. It seemed to Louise as if he'd been *expecting* them.

"Did you enjoy my special candies?" Mr. Webster asked, not looking up from his task. His voice was steady and quiet, and Louise almost wished he'd shout and rant and leap up and down, rather than stay this calm. It just didn't feel right.

"They were really nice," Louise lied. She didn't want to risk upsetting him any more than they already had.

"You don't sound very convincing to me," Mr. Webster replied, still not looking up, and still speaking in the same quiet, controlled voice.

Louise could feel her spine stiffening. "Really, Mr. Webster, they were —"

"Sorry, Mr. Webster," Niki interrupted, "but the truth is that they were a bit of a letdown. It was like having a load of sawdust in your mouth." Louise looked at her in amazement. That was the last thing they needed — Niki giving him attitude.

"What a shame," Mr. Webster replied. He emptied the contents of his dustpan into a big plastic bag.

"We're really, really sorry, Mr. Webster," Louise said in a rush. "We shouldn't have taken them in the first place."

Mr. Webster paused, stood up, and stared at the three girls. It felt to Louise like he was looking straight through them.

"Yes, you are correct," he said at last.

"Um . . ." Louise began, "is our friend Sarah still here?"

"She's in the kitchen helping me fix all the damage you've done." Louise thought she saw a glint in the storekeeper's eyes.

"Are you going to report us to the police?" Laura asked shakily.

Louise swallowed, but her throat felt really dry. She looked at Niki. The look of defiance from earlier had drained away, along with the color in her face.

"I'm not going to report you," he replied. Louise felt relief, even though she really wasn't feeling well at all. "But there is one condition. You've all got to help me, too."

That seems fair, Louise thought. *Just a few hours' work, a little stirring and sweeping, and this will all be over*. She turned to see Laura nod and Niki mumble her agreement. They both looked as white as sheets.

"OK, Mr. Webster," Louise said. "We'll give you a hand."

"Follow me, girls." He turned and shuffled off toward the large kitchen door.

As they entered the kitchen, an extremely odd feeling overtook Louise. Her forehead and her back began sweating, and her mouth felt numb — like when she'd gone to the dentist to have a filling. But there was a strange tingling feeling, as if someone were sticking tiny pins into her lips. She ran her tongue over them. They were icy cold, and it felt as if all the nerves around her mouth were stiffening up. She began to rub her jaw with one hand and press her fingers to her lips with the other. It was strange how the numbness felt even worse than the tingling. She turned her head to see that both Laura and Niki were rubbing their jaws, too. She could feel the blood racing behind her eyes. Panic was setting in.

What was happening?

She dug her fingernails into her lips, desperate to feel something other than the terrifying, frozen nothingness. Frantically, she turned back to Niki and Laura.

How could they all be feeling like this? What had they eaten . . . ?

Webster's Specials!

Her stomach turned over. Cold, sick terror swirled inside her.

In the dim light of the kitchen, Sarah was sitting on a high stool with her back to the others, whisking something in a large metal bowl. The whirring and grinding noise of machinery clattered around them. Mr. Webster's kitchen seemed less like a kitchen and more like some sort of laboratory.

"Sarah." Louise managed to move her stiff, numb mouth. Sarah didn't turn around. With a huge effort, Louise shouted even louder. "*Sarah!*" Tentatively, she raised a hand and tapped her friend on the shoulder.

"Sarah —"

Louise froze. Even in the half-light, she could see that Sarah's eyes were dark with sadness and her pale cheeks streaked with tears. And then Louise saw why Sarah hadn't answered.

Sarah no longer had a mouth! Only a thin red line where her lips had been . . .

Louise watched in horror as Sarah tried to form words, but no sound came out at all — except a low nasal whine. For all of Sarah's frantic efforts, her mouth remained sealed.

Louise recoiled, crashing against a high metal table. Her lips were quickly tightening, and she was becoming dizzy and faint. She had to get out of this kitchen *now*. She turned around, frantically looking for Niki and Laura. *They all had to get out!*

But as she saw Niki and Laura, the blood in her veins turned to ice. Niki had fallen to her knees, and Laura was huddled beside her, blue eyes wide and staring in confusion.

They no longer had mouths, either.

Louise tried to cry out, but her teeth felt as though they were being welded together. She could only manage a dull whimper.

Slowly, knowing what she would find, Louise raised her hand to her own mouth — or rather, to the space in her face where her mouth no longer was. . . .

GOOD LUCK,
BAD LUCK

Your grandma's not really all there, is she?"

Thirteen-year-old Greg Cranston and his best friend, Sam Drake, were walking home after school on the Friday afternoon before spring break.

Greg stopped in his tracks at Sam's words and stared at him. Sam was right. Greg's grandmother was a little forgetful nowadays, but it wasn't something that he felt comfortable talking about.

Sam gave an apologetic smile. "Sorry," he said. "But from what you've told me about her, she can't be."

"She's old, that's all," Greg said, frowning as he kept on walking. "She's got arthritis, and she has trouble with her balance — and she only forgets things once in a while."

"You said she doesn't even know who you are sometimes when you visit her in that nursing home," Sam said. Greg could tell he was fascinated by the whole thing.

Greg grimaced. "OK, so she forgets things," he said. "She gets confused and scared. It happens to lots of people her age."

"Maybe," Sam said, "but she's only two years older than my grandma — and my grandma went skiing in Colorado last year." He looked at Greg. "How long has she been in that home?"

Greg thought back. He had no memory of his grandmother in any other place. His father had told him that years and years ago the nursing home had been a lunatic asylum. Greg found the idea of that a little creepy.

"It's like she's been there forever," he said, scratching at his short, spiky brown hair. "But she wasn't always this bad. We used to take her around the gardens in a wheelchair a few years back. But she doesn't leave her room at all now." He looked at Sam. His friend's bright blue eyes were sympathetic under his unruly tangle of blonde hair.

"That sounds pretty bad," Sam said.

Greg nodded. "Her arthritis has gotten so bad that she hardly ever gets out of bed," he continued. "She can't read or knit or do crosswords or puzzles or any of that kind of thing. So she just sits there in bed, watching television all the time. And she's getting a lot more frightened and confused these days. Sometimes when we visit her, she just stares at the walls — I don't know — as if she's seeing things that aren't really there." He glanced at Sam. "Things that scare her."

"What kind of things?" Sam asked.

Greg shrugged. "Beats me," he said. "She looks around the room as if she thinks there are monsters hiding behind the furniture. And she freaks out if you make any sudden noises."

"How often do you visit her?" Sam asked.

"Two or three times a month," Greg replied. "I know this must sound really mean, Sam . . . but I wish I didn't have to go. It's totally miserable there. And it's not like

Grandma gets anything out of it, even when she remembers who we are. And it's gotten worse since Grandpa died."

Sam looked at him. "You got along really well with your grandpa, didn't you?"

Greg nodded. His grandfather had died six weeks ago. It was completely unexpected. The doctors said a heart attack was to blame.

The visits to the nursing home only got worse after that. Greg's grandfather wasn't there to remind his grandmother who people were. Now she thought her own relatives were just a bunch of strangers who came into her room sometimes.

"So, what are we going to do next week?" Sam asked, breaking into Greg's gloomy thoughts. "You know, spring break?"

Greg smiled. They had a whole week to themselves.

"I don't know," he said. "But I think I deserve some fun after the last few weeks." He thought for a second. "I'd like to go to the movies, and there's a new computer game and other stuff that I want. But I've spent all my pocket money, so I don't know if I'll be able to get anything."

"I'm flat broke, too," Sam said. "We'll just have to find cheap things to do — unless we can make some quick cash."

They were still talking about their plans when they arrived at Greg's front lawn.

As they walked up the path, the front door was thrown open, and Greg's little sister, Edie, appeared on the step, her long auburn hair hanging over her pointy face. She grinned at them.

"I know something you don't!" she said. Then she slammed the front door shut, with both boys still outside.

"Edie?" Greg called. But there was no reply. "EDIE!"

Greg and Sam looked at each other. "She's nuts," Sam said.

Greg didn't see much of Edie these days. When he'd been younger, they had played together a lot, but over the past couple of years Greg had outgrown her. After all, when Greg was hanging out with his friends, the last thing he needed was his little sister tagging along. It wasn't fun, and it *certainly* wasn't cool.

He pulled the front door key out of his pocket, and he and Sam went inside.

"You have to hear that new album I told you about," Greg said. "You'll love it. It's really great."

"It can't be better than their first one," Sam said. "Not possible."

"It is," said Greg, grinning. "Trust me. It's amazing."

Edie was squatting halfway up the stairs, waiting for them.

"I know something you don't know," she said.

"You already said that," Greg responded as he closed the front door. "What do you think you know?"

"You'll find out." Edie turned and scrambled up the stairs and vanished around the corner in a flurry of legs. A moment later, her bedroom door banged shut.

Greg's mother's voice came from the kitchen. "Hey! Less noise, please!"

"It was Edie," Greg called.

"Greg? Aha! You're just the person I want. Come on in, sweetie."

Sam nudged Greg. "Sweetie?"

"Shut up," Greg replied.

His mother's face appeared at the kitchen doorway. "And Sam, too. That's perfect. How's it going, Sam? Are you feeling strong today?"

"I'm fine, thanks, Mrs. Cranston," said Sam, sounding puzzled.

"Great." She beckoned them in. "I've got a little proposition for the two of you."

Greg and Sam went into the sunlit kitchen.

"How would you boys like to do a good deed and make a little money?" Mrs. Cranston asked.

"The money sounds interesting, Mom," Greg said with a smile. "But I'm not so sure about the good deed." He went to the fridge and got out two cans of Coke. "Good deeds are usually hard work." He grinned at her. "What are you proposing?"

"Grandpa's house is going to be sold," Mrs. Cranston said. "We've arranged for some professional movers to come in and take away all the furniture, but there are a lot of personal things in there that need to be carefully packed up first." She looked at Greg and Sam. "So — what do you say? I'll make it worth your while. I know Greg's been wanting a new computer game, and I bet you've got a long shopping list, too, Sam. How does fifty dollars each sound?"

Sam's eyes lit up and he nodded enthusiastically. "That sounds very fair to me! What do you think, Greg?"

"There you go, Greg," his mom said. "Sam's up for it. It'll only take you a couple of days. Three at the most. And you'd be helping out me and your dad. We'd do it, but you know your dad has that conference to go to, and I'm busy in the store."

Greg's father ran a company that organized large-scale meetings and conferences all over the country. It meant he had to be away from home a lot. His mom owned a flower shop that was open seven days a week, and during this time of year she had to be there nearly every day.

Working over in Grandpa's house certainly hadn't been one of the things he'd planned for that week. However, the money sounded good, and if they worked really fast, he and Sam might be able to get it done in a day or so.

"You'll have to explain exactly what you want us to do," Greg said to his mom.

"I've already made you a list," she said. "A bundle of cardboard boxes are being delivered there in the morning. All you have to do is fill them up and write on the outside with a marker, so we know what's in each one."

"OK," Greg said. "When do you want us to start?"

"Tomorrow would be great," Greg's mom replied. "The moving men are coming to take the furniture away on Tuesday, and I really want all your grandpa's personal stuff gone by then."

"You up for starting tomorrow?" Greg asked Sam.

"Why not?"

Greg grinned at his mother. "Do we get paid up front?"

She laughed. "You can have some pizza money now — and the rest when you finish."

"Awesome." He looked at Sam. "Let's go up to my room," he said. "There are a couple of tracks on the new album that are going to totally blow your mind."

They left the kitchen and headed upstairs.

"Did your grandpa have a lot of stuff?" Sam asked.

"Not tons," Greg said. "There are loads of rooms, but he only lived in about three or four of them. It's a really old house, so you never know. We might even find some valuable antiques."

"Do I get a share if we do?" Sam asked.

"Fifty-fifty," Greg laughed. *Clearing out Grandpa's things might actually turn out to be OK*, he thought. He didn't say it out loud, but he also hoped that spending time in the old house might somehow help him come to terms with losing his grandfather. He hadn't been there since the family and friends had come for a bite to eat after the funeral a month ago. And that had been really grim.

They were halfway up the stairs when Greg's mother appeared in the hallway.

"Oh, I forgot to mention," she said. "Edie will be helping you as well. So I want you to keep an eye on her and make sure she behaves herself. And when you go for food, take her with you, please. She won't be any trouble. She's promised to behave herself and to do what she's told."

Having said that, she went back into the kitchen.

Greg and Sam looked at each other in horror.

"I don't believe it," Sam said. "Your mom's set us up."

From the landing above them, they heard the sound of Edie's bedroom door open. There was a cackle like fingernails down a blackboard. Then the door slammed shut again.

Now they knew what Edie had meant when she said she knew something they didn't.

This was going to be a total nightmare.

—

Now, Edie, I want you to listen to me," said Mrs. Cranston, bending down to look square into her daughter's eyes. "I want you to behave yourself and do what your brother tells you, OK?"

"Yes, Mom," Edie replied.

Greg, Sam, and Edie were standing on the sidewalk outside the wide wrought-iron gate of Grandpa's house.

"And don't race around like a little puppy, and *please* try not to break anything." She turned to Greg and Sam. "And you'll remember to pack the heavy things at the bottom and the fragile things on the top, right?"

"Of course, Mom," Greg replied.

His mom smiled. "Look after her."

Greg nodded.

"Greg's in charge," his mom said as she started up the car engine. "Remember that, Edie!"

"Yes, Mom," Edie said meekly.

"Bye-bye," Mrs. Cranston said. "You've got my cell phone number if there are any problems, and you can reach me at the store till twelve, OK? And I'll be over this afternoon to see how you're doing."

She drove along the curved, tree-shaded road and was gone.

Greg turned to his sister. "You're going to do what I tell you, got it?" he said firmly.

She gave him a withering look. "In your dreams," she said.

"Edie!"

"You're not my boss," she said, pushing the gate open. "Where are the keys?"

"In my pocket."

"Give them to me."

"No."

Edie glared at him. She took out her cell phone. "Give them to me *right now*, or I'll call Mom and tell her you're being a total jerk."

Greg took the keys from his pocket and dropped them into her hand. "Fine," he said. "Take them. What do I care? Just stay out of our way, OK?"

Edie went racing up the path between the rhododendron bushes.

"Way to keep her under control," Sam said, laughing.

"Trust me on this," Greg said. "It's going to be easier if we just let her do what she wants. If we try to tell her what to do, it'll turn into a war. With any luck, she'll go off somewhere and spend the morning chatting with her dopey friends on her cell phone."

"Just so long as she doesn't invite them over," Sam said.

Greg stared at him in alarm. "Don't even *think* that!" he said.

They walked up the path. The big old, green-painted door was wide open and led into the familiar hallway. But Greg could see that there were already less familiar things in there.

The hallway was filled with flat-packed piles of cardboard boxes, rolls of brown tape, and stacks of white packing paper.

"Smells a little funny in here," Sam said, still standing on the doormat.

Greg walked into the hallway. "This is the way it always smells," he said.

It gave Greg a strange, hollow feeling to look at his grandpa's things again. All he remembered about the last visit to the house after the funeral was being totally miserable and wishing Grandpa had been there to say something funny and make him laugh.

But there was nobody here to tell funny stories. There was just a big, old, empty house full of stuff that didn't belong to anyone anymore.

Greg looked around at his grandfather's things. The old upright piano that no one played. The two-seater couch with the wicker back and the seat covers with the huge red flowers on them. The leather footstool. The big old table with the four chairs. And the faded and worn leather armchair he used to sit in.

"This is just like a museum," Sam said, gazing around.

"My mom said that Grandpa didn't change anything after my grandmother went into the home. He left it all like this so he'd remember her better, I guess."

"Old people do strange stuff sometimes," Sam said. He glanced at Greg. "Sorry — I didn't mean your grandpa was strange."

"He wasn't," Greg said, more sharply than he meant. "He just missed Grandma."

Sam homed in on an ancient record player with a

dusty black lid. There were boxes of vinyl LPs nearby.

"Wow! State-of-the-art sound system!" Sam said with a grin. He lifted the lid. "I wonder if it works." He looked at Greg. "What kind of music did he listen to? Classical stuff, or what?"

"Take a look for yourself," Greg said, nodding toward the row of boxes along the wall. "They're in alphabetical order."

Sam opened one of the boxes and pulled out an LP. "'Manuel and His Music of the Mountains,'" he read from a cover that showed a picture of snowcapped mountains. "I bet it's killer." He pulled out more albums. "James Last? Mantovani? Felix Mendelssohn?" He shook his head. "I've never heard of *any* of these people."

"Mozart's Symphony in G," Greg read. "There you go — you must have heard of Mozart."

"I bet he doesn't get downloaded too often," Sam chuckled. "Let's see if it works — just for a laugh."

Greg felt a twinge of disloyalty. It seemed wrong to make fun of his grandfather's music like that, but he slid an LP out of its cover and put it on the turntable.

He pressed a switch, and moments later a scratchy noise came out of the speakers — followed by a blast of orchestral music.

Sam stood up, grinning from ear to ear. "That's really bad," he laughed.

"True," Greg admitted, smiling in spite of himself. "Old people have such weird taste in music."

Greg leaned over the turntable and switched it off. He watched as the needle arm lifted. The scratchy music stopped. Greg stood up. "Come on — we need to get going or we'll be here all week."

They went out into the hall and dragged a pile of flat boxes into the living room. Sam assembled them, and Greg secured the bottoms with the brown tape. Soon they had quite a pile ready to be packed.

"Where did your sister go?" Sam asked.

"Don't know. Don't care," Greg said. "Just so long as she keeps out of our way, she can do what she wants. OK — where do we start?"

"Heavy stuff at the bottom," Sam said. He walked over to the piano and picked up a statuette of an elephant. "This is pretty heavy."

"OK, wrap it in tissue and stick it in the box," Greg said.

"It's all dusty and filthy," Sam said with a grimace. "Everything's covered in dust. And there are cobwebs and all kinds of grime down the back of this piano."

"Don't look," Greg said. "Just think of the money."

A loud crash from directly above made them both jump.

Greg stared up at the ceiling. "Oh, no! Edie!" he groaned.

"You *were* told to keep an eye on her," Sam said helpfully.

Greg gave him an exasperated look. "We'd better go and see what she's done."

They headed up the stairs and onto the landing. One door was open at the far end of the hallway. It was the door of the room directly above the living room.

"Edie?" Greg shouted. "What are you doing?"

"It wasn't my fault," came Edie's voice from inside the room. "It just fell."

Edie was in a big room with a pale red carpet and floral wallpaper. There was a big double bed with a

51

rose-patterned comforter. Two night tables. A dressing table with three mirrors. A chest of drawers. Two big armoires.

Greg immediately saw what had smashed. A full-length mirror on a polished wooden stand lay facedown on the carpet. Shards of glass were scattered across the floor. Edie was standing as far away from it as possible, her face sullen and defiant. "It just fell," she said.

"On its own, I bet," said Greg sarcastically. "What were you doing?"

"Nothing," Edie said. "It's *not* my fault."

"That's seven years' bad luck," Sam said, peering over Greg's shoulder. "Breaking a mirror."

"It's not!" Edie said. "Anyway . . . I didn't break it. It fell."

The mirror had fallen in front of an armoire. Arranged along the top of the armoire was a collection of dolls with porcelain faces and old-fashioned clothes. One doll was missing from the row. It was lying facedown on the carpet.

"You were climbing on it to try and get at the dolls, weren't you?" Greg said.

"No."

"You're such a liar, Edie," Greg said. "Go and see if you can find a broom and a dustpan in the kitchen."

Edie shoved past them and hammered her way down the stairs.

"Great," Greg said, sighing. "Mom will go ballistic when she sees this. And it's probably a really valuable antique or something. That girl is a human wrecking ball."

Between them, Greg and Sam managed to lift the mirror in its heavy wooden frame. Only the top part of the mirror was actually shattered; the rest of it was still held in the frame. They picked up the fragments of glass and put them in the hearth of the fireplace.

"Where is your sister with that broom and dustpan?" Sam asked.

"Oh, she's probably off somewhere sulking," Greg said. "But it doesn't matter. Guess who'll get the blame?"

Sam opened the door to the armoire with the dolls. "There's something in the bottom," Sam said as he leaned in and pulled it out.

Greg went over to look.

It was a piece of thick cardstock, folded in two and held together with some green tape.

"What is it?" Greg asked. "It looks like some kind of game board — you know, like for Monopoly or something."

Sam crouched on the carpet and carefully opened the thing. "I don't think so," he said. "I think it's a map."

Greg knelt at his side, leaning close to have a better look.

The map was amazingly detailed and beautifully drawn in colors that had faded over the years. Woods and open land were in greens; streets and paths in yellows and grays; buildings in soft red tints or in shades of brown.

All around the map, the same phrase was repeated over and over again: MAKE YOUR OWN LUCK. MAKE YOUR OWN LUCK. MAKE YOUR OWN LUCK. . . .

"Oh, wow!" Greg breathed. "It's not just a map; it's a map of *here*." He pointed at a green space. "Look, that's the park — and there's Saint Matthew's Church. And the center of town." But there were things that were different — and things that were missing as well. "Where's our school?" he wondered aloud.

"The shopping center's not there, either," said Sam. "The big parking garage is missing, too."

"Hey, you know what this is, don't you?" Greg said. "It's a map of how the town looked in the past." He leaned in even closer. "Look! It's got this house on it."

Sure enough, there it was on the map — except that on the map there was no park next to it. There was just open woodland.

Greg traced his finger along the path that led from the center of town, through the woods, and right up to the front door of the house. But it was not quite like the other streets and paths shown on the map. It was divided into squares, and for some reason, the map-maker had given each square its own particular color. Greg followed the path to the house. It ended at the front door. Written on the doorstep was the word START.

Sam looked closely at the colored path. "There are tiny little things drawn on it," he said. "See? There's a different one on each square. Weird."

"There's writing on some of the squares, too," Greg said. "You know what this is, don't you? It *is* a board game! Is there anything else in the closet? Instructions or anything?"

Sam delved into the armoire again. "Yes!" he said.

It was a small wooden box with a sliding lid. A piece

of paper had been glued to the lid and on it, in old-fashioned, faded, ornate lettering, were the words GOOD LUCK, BAD LUCK.

Inside the box was a pack of yellowing playing cards held together by a piece of knotted ribbon. There was also a pair of dice, a small wooden cup, and a tattered booklet. Sam lifted the booklet out of the box. "Hey, look at these," he said. Underneath lay two little wooden figures.

Greg picked up the two figures and stood them on the board. They were roughly human-shaped, but without much detail. The body of one showed small patches of blue paint; the other had once been painted red. The faces were totally blank — with no features at all.

"I think all this stuff is handmade and hand-painted," Greg said, twisting one of the figures in his fingers. He picked up the booklet and opened it. There seemed to be instructions and rules written inside, but they were written by hand in ink that had faded so much it was lilac-colored on the browned pages.

"Do you think your grandpa or grandma might have made it?" Sam asked. "You know — when they were kids, maybe?"

"It's possible, I suppose," Greg said. "I don't know that Grandma has ever been artistic like that, but Grandpa used to be a jeweler, so he'd be able to make detailed stuff like the writing on those little squares, I guess." He frowned. "But why didn't he ever show it to me? I'd tell the whole world if I'd created something like that."

Each square had its own tiny painted object on it. A horseshoe. A pair of magpies. A ladder. A clover leaf. A knife. A crescent moon. A well. A rabbit. A gold ring. A frog. A goblet. A shining star. And every now and then, there was a yellowish square with tiny words written on it: DRAW A CARD.

"Well, the rules seem pretty straightforward," Sam said as he thumbed through the booklet. "There's a lot here, but basically, you start at the house and throw the dice. Whatever number comes up, that's how many squares you move. If you land on one of the yellow squares, you have to pick a card from the top of the deck." He looked at Greg. "There's not much to it, really."

"Doesn't it say anything about what the drawings on the squares mean?" Greg asked.

"I'm not sure. Some of the writing is a little tricky to read."

Greg picked up the pack of cards. The knot on the ribbon wouldn't come loose, so he carefully eased the cards out of the stiff loop. Written on the back of each card were the words DO YOU FEEL LUCKY?

Greg was about to turn over the top card to see what was written on the underside when Sam's hand came down on his to stop him. "No, you don't," Sam said. "The rules specifically forbid any player from looking at the cards in advance." He nodded toward the rule book. "And it says that players have to forfeit a turn if they break any of the rules."

"Technically, I'm not playing yet," Greg said.

"Well, that's not exactly true," Sam said with a wide grin. "Look — it says right here on the first page that the game begins when the board is opened up." He laughed. "Whether you like it or not, we're already playing."

"So let's play," Greg said.

There was the sound of stomping feet on the landing.

"Edie." Greg groaned. For someone who was all skin and bone, his sister certainly had a loud way of letting you know she was around. "If she sees us with this game, she'll want to join in."

"So, let her," said Sam. "What's the problem?"

"Edie is a total monster with board games," Greg said. "She always cheats and she sulks like crazy if she doesn't win. This is *really* old — like, kind of an antique, right? If Edie gets her hands on it, she'll probably wreck it."

"So tell her to get lost," Sam suggested.

"Oh, sure — *that'll* work!" Greg replied. "Hang on, though. There's a bolt on the door!" He ran across the room and pushed the bolt in place. A moment later, the door handle rattled.

"Open this door!" Edie shouted.

"No. Go away," Greg replied. Sam stifled a laugh.

The handle rattled furiously. "Let me in! Why's the door locked? What are you doing in there?"

"Nothing," Greg called. "We're cleaning up the glass from the broken mirror. Get lost, Edie. You've made enough trouble. You're not coming in."

The door shook as Edie kicked it. "I'm telling Mom on you!"

"Go ahead," Greg called. "And I'll tell her about the mirror you broke!"

"Pig!" She stomped away. Greg and Sam looked at each other and grinned.

"That got rid of her," Greg said, kneeling down by the board. "OK — you start."

Sam picked up the dice and put them in the little wooden cup. He shook them for a few moments, then let them spill out onto the board. "Three and two," he said. "That's five. I'll be blue." He picked up the wooden figure and walked it down five squares of the path from the house. "I've landed on a horseshoe." He frowned. "Is that good luck or bad luck? I can't remember."

"I'm pretty sure it's good luck," Greg said.

Sam smiled. "Excellent."

Greg frowned. "Is there anything in the rules about what actually *happens* when you land on a good-luck square? Do you get an extra turn or something?"

"I don't think so," Sam said. He handed Greg the booklet. "You read it."

Greg flipped through the pages. "Maybe we should do this later," he said. He looked at his watch. "We've been here nearly an hour, and we haven't packed up a single thing. Mom will kill us if we don't get busy."

"What about the game?" Sam asked.

"Just leave it here for now."

They got up and Greg unbolted the door. They made their way downstairs to the living room. Edie was stretched out on the couch chatting on her cell phone.

"You're supposed to be helping!" Greg said to her.

"Just a sec, Hailey," Edie said into the phone. She glared at Greg. "I'm talking to my friend," she said. "You are *so* rude!"

"Let's just work around her," Sam suggested.

"If you're not going to be helpful, can you just go somewhere else?" Greg said to Edie.

With irritating slowness, Edie got up off the couch and slouched out of the room, talking on the phone all the while.

"And don't break anything else!" Greg called after her.

For the next hour or so, Greg and Sam worked quickly and methodically. They wrapped the heavier things and placed them in the bottom of the boxes, then they used scrunched-up tissue paper to make a bedding for the next layer of stuff. The boxes gradually filled up and were taped down and labeled with the marker:

LIVING-ROOM ORNAMENTS OFF THE MANTELPIECE.

LIVING-ROOM FRAMED PHOTOS.

Sam was standing on a chair to reach ornaments on the top shelf of the bookcase when he let out a low whistle.

"What?" Greg asked. He was hot and dusty and sweaty.

"Look at what I found!" Sam said. He turned, waving a ten-dollar bill. "It was in this." In his other hand, he held a shiny china mug with a red horseshoe painted on the side.

"Well, lucky you," said a voice from the door. They both turned. Greg's mother stood there, smiling. "You boys have been busy," she said. "I'm impressed."

"What time is it?" Greg asked.

"Half-past one."

The time had raced by; Greg had no idea it was so late. Sam climbed down off the chair and offered the ten-dollar bill to Greg's mother.

She smiled. "No, you found it," she said. "You can keep it, Sam."

A huge grin spread over Sam's face. "Thanks, Mrs. Cranston," he said. He looked at Greg. "That horseshoe did give me good luck after all," he said.

"What horseshoe?" Greg's mom asked.

"We found a game — Grandma and Grandpa's board game," Greg explained. "The one with the map of our town and everything."

Mrs. Cranston frowned. "I don't know what you mean, Greg."

"It's upstairs. I'll go and get it."

"I'll go up with you," said his mother. "I wanted to take a look around the bedroom. There might be a few things I'd like as keepsakes. Grandma had a wonderful collection of antique dolls. They're certainly not going to any charity store."

Greg looked uneasily at her. "There's been a tiny

accident," he said. "There was a big mirror — on a stand. It got . . . broken."

"Oh, that's a shame," said his mother. "But it's my fault. I should have told you to leave the bedroom till I arrived. The frame for that mirror has always been a little rickety. I hope no one got hurt." She looked around. "Where's Edie?" she asked.

"She's around somewhere," Greg said. "Last time I saw her, she was on her cell phone."

Greg's mom shook her head. "I told your father giving her a phone of her own was a bad idea," she said. She looked at them. "OK, show me this game you mentioned, and then maybe we can all drive to town for some food before we start work again."

They went up to the bedroom. Mrs. Cranston's eyes widened as she caught sight of the game. "What a fabulous thing," she breathed as she knelt down on the carpet and gazed at the board. "I've never seen it before. I wonder where it's from. I've seen old maps of the local area. This must have been made at least a hundred years ago. And look at all the detail! It's beautiful!"

"I know," Greg said. "And it all looks handmade, too."

64

"I'm the blue piece," Sam said, pointing at the figure that was still standing on the board. "See? I landed on the square with the horseshoe on it. And then I went downstairs and found the money in that mug with the horseshoe on it."

"That's quite a coincidence," Mrs. Cranston said, smiling. Her eyes twinkled as she looked at him. "Or is it, I wonder . . ."

"You've *got* to be kidding," said Greg, exasperated. "You don't really think this game had anything to do with it, do you?"

His mother laughed. "No, of course not." She got up. "But it's beautifully crafted. We should definitely keep it. Let's carefully pack it all up now and put it back into the armoire for safekeeping. I'll have to ask Grandma about it next time we go over there." She looked at the two friends. "OK," she said. "I think it's time the workers had a lunch break. Let's go down and find Edie, and then get ourselves something to eat."

"Sam can pay for his own with that money he found," Greg laughed.

"Hey!" Sam said. "No way!"

"Don't worry, Sam," Mrs. Cranston said, putting her

arm around his shoulders. "I'm paying. You keep those ten dollars. After all, it was your good luck that you found it."

After lunch, Greg's mom drove them all back to the house for a few more hours' work. Mrs. Cranston took Edie with her upstairs, leaving the two boys to finish packing up the living room.

"At least, she'll have to do some actual work now," Greg said as he watched Edie follow his mother up the stairs.

Greg and Sam carried the filled and labeled boxes out and piled them along one wall in the wide hallway.

"Mom?" Greg called up the stairs. "What's next?"

"I'm on my way," his mother called.

She came down the stairs carrying a box in her arms.

"I've got all of Grandma's dolls and I'm going to take them home," Greg's mom said. "Edie's coming with me. I think she's had enough for today. Haven't you, honey?"

"Yes, Mom." Edie gave Greg a look of triumph. "Haven't I been really helpful?"

"Yes, you have, sweetie," her mother said.

"She didn't lift a finger this morning," Greg protested.

His mother looked at him. "Well, whose fault is that?" she said cheerfully. "I left you in charge of her."

Greg knew there was no point in arguing about it. The more angry he got, the more Edie would gloat.

"Are we all finished for the day?" Greg asked.

"I think so," said his mother. "I'll tell you what, how about the two of you take a look at what needs to be done in the kitchen while I drive Edie over to Hailey's house. Then I'll come back for you, and we'll call it a day."

Sam and Greg helped Mrs. Cranston slide the big box of dolls onto the backseat of the car while Edie clambered into the passenger seat. As they drove off, Edie stuck her tongue out at Greg and Sam through the open window.

"I really wish I had a little sister," Sam said with a fake sigh and a wide grin. "It must be *so* great."

"Take mine," Greg said as they turned to go back into the house. "I'll sell her to you for that cash you found."

"Not a chance," Sam said with a laugh. "But wasn't that amazing, though? Finding the money like that — and in a mug with a horseshoe on it, too. Talk about Creepsville."

"It's not Creepsville," Greg said. "It was just a coincidence."

"Pete says you should always keep an open mind about stuff like that," Sam said. Pete was Sam's seventeen-year-old brother.

"I wouldn't pay too much attention to what Pete has to say," said Greg. "His mind is so open that his brain keeps falling out."

"Oh, ha-ha," muttered Sam sarcastically. "All the same — I'm going to perform an experiment with that game. I'm going to find out if landing on a lucky square really does work." He ran along the hall and bounded up the stairs two at a time.

"Hey — what are you doing?" Greg called.

"I'm taking another turn!" Sam said.

Greg ran up the stairs after him.

He found Sam standing in the bedroom doorway, staring at the floor over by the armoire.

"That's weird," Sam said.

"What?"

"Look!" Greg peered over Sam's shoulder. They had put away the game in the bottom of the armoire. . . .

But it was out again.

Sam's blue man was back on the board — standing in the horseshoe square. Beside the board, the wooden cup waited with the two dice in it.

"Mom and Edie must have taken it out again," Greg said.

"And set it up exactly the same as it was?" Sam said, a questioning tone in his voice.

Greg shrugged and pushed past him. "It's not your turn, don't forget," Greg said. "It's mine."

"It would be if we were playing by the rules," Sam pointed out. "But we're not." He scooped up the wooden cup.

"Ow!" he exclaimed, dropping the cup immediately. Greg saw that by some fluke it had landed upright on the carpet with the two dice still inside it. Sam sucked his finger.

"What's up?" Greg asked.

"I got a splinter, I think," Sam said.

"Serves you right," smiled Greg. He picked up the cup and looked carefully at it. "But I don't see how," he said. "It's completely smooth."

"I'm telling you that it's a splinter," Sam complained. "Look." He showed Greg his finger. There was a bead of blood on the end. "Perhaps it was payback for trying to skip your turn," he grinned. "Maybe the game doesn't like it when people don't obey the rules."

"Oh, please!" Greg said with a laugh. "It's just a board game."

"It's your turn," Sam said. "Roll the dice."

He tipped the cup and the dice rolled out over the board. "Ten," he said. "Not bad. It beats you, anyway." He took the red man out of the box and walked it ten squares from the house.

He looked closely at the picture on the square where he had landed.

"It's a ladder," he said. "And there's someone falling off it."

"That's got to be a bad-luck square," Sam said with a frown. "You'd better keep far away from ladders for a while."

"You're a total nutcase, you know?" Greg said. "There's no way that this game could give you good luck or bad. It doesn't make sense." He put the dice back into the cup. "Anyway, it's your turn."

"No thanks," Sam said. "Not until I'm sure you're not going to fall off a ladder. I don't want to risk it."

Greg laughed. "I can't believe you're being such an idiot about this," he said.

Sam just shook his head, his face unsmiling.

"Oh, suit yourself," said Greg. "Let's pack it away and go and take a look at the kitchen."

They carefully stowed the game away in the bottom of the armoire and headed back downstairs.

All they had time to do in the kitchen before Greg's mom arrived was pack a few boxes.

"At this rate, you'll be finished tomorrow," she said. "It's not so bad, is it?" She peered out through the kitchen window into the yard. "It's like the wilderness out there. I might hire someone to clean up the place before we start showing it to potential buyers." She ran a finger across the pane, leaving a clear trail in the fine dust. "And these windows might benefit the most." She looked at Greg. "Your grandfather kept a stepladder in the cellar. Would you mind carrying it up tomorrow and giving the windows a quick scrub?"

Greg could see that Sam was staring at him. He turned to his mother. "A stepladder?" he said uneasily, in spite of himself.

"Yes. You won't be able to reach otherwise," said his mother. "But I'm happy to do it myself if you don't like the idea."

"Uh . . . no," Greg said. "It's not a problem. I'll do it."

No way was he going to allow Sam to freak him out about that game. And no way in the world was he going to fall off that stepladder tomorrow.

Things like that just *didn't* happen.

Greg and Sam had their evening nicely planned out: Chinese food and a DVD rental to watch at Sam's place. His parents were going out for the evening. His brother would be in the house but, knowing Pete, he'd be up in his attic bedroom, busy with his PC — which meant they'd have the run of the living room and the use of the wide-screen TV.

It was just beginning to get dark as Greg and Sam

arrived in the center of town. They propped their bikes against the wall outside the Chinese takeout place and went in to give their order. While the food was being prepared, they headed across the street.

"What movie do you want?" Greg asked as they browsed the shelves.

"*Slash and Burn* is supposed to be really good," Sam said. "Pete's watched it, and he says it's great. But I can't see it here. I'll go and ask."

They headed off to the counter.

"You're in luck," said the assistant, reaching under the counter and bringing out a DVD. "It was just returned. All the other copies are out right now. It's our most popular movie this week."

Sam grinned at Greg as he handed over the rental money. "See?" he said. "*My* luck is still holding out."

Greg laughed. "Yeah — right."

They went back to the restaurant. They had to wait for a few minutes before they were handed a warm bag filled with cartons of food.

"I'm sure there's more in here than we ordered," Sam murmured as they came out onto the street. He opened the bag. "Yes, there is. Look, it's written on each carton! There's a whole extra special rice and an order of sweet-and-sour pork." He looked at Greg. "Wow! Isn't that amazing? Two things we didn't pay for."

Greg stared into the takeout bag. This was getting weird. Unless Sam's run of good luck ended pretty soon, Greg was going to start wondering about that Good Luck, Bad Luck game.

He moved toward where they had left their bikes. "I just hope some of your luck rubs off on me," he said, his head turned over his shoulder toward Sam.

"Hey! Watch out!"

The voice from above startled him. He turned his head just in time to see the edge of a metal ladder looming right in front of his eyes.

For a moment or two, he saw stars. A fierce pain shot through his head and he staggered backward and fell against the wall.

Dazed and hurt, Greg was vaguely aware of the sound of someone coming down the ladder. "You could have killed me!" said the voice. "Why don't you watch where you're going?" The tone of the voice changed to concern. "Did you get hurt?"

Greg had his hand to his head. He blinked at the man standing over him.

"What?" he gasped.

"Are you OK?" asked the man.

Greg noticed that Sam was staring at him with his mouth half open.

"Yes," Greg said, pulling himself together. "I'm fine." He stared at the ladder. Where had that come from? It hadn't been there when they'd gone into the restaurant.

"That's a stupid place to put a ladder," he mumbled.

"What?" The man stared at him. "I can't put up a ladder in front of my own store to replace a lightbulb?"

Sam looked at Greg. "Are you all right?" he asked. "You really got whacked."

Greg blinked at him. "Is there blood?"

Sam peered close. "No," he said. "But there'll be a massive bruise, I bet."

"Stupid ladder!" Greg said.

Sam stared at him with an uneasy look on his face.

"What?" Greg said.

"The ladder!" Sam said. "Don't you get it?"

"Yes, I got it," Greg said. "Right between the eyes."

"No! The *game!*" said Sam. "The square you landed

on had a picture of a ladder on it . . . and you've just walked into a ladder!"

Greg looked at him. "To start," he said, "the picture was of someone falling *off* a ladder — and no one fell off the ladder. And the idea that I walked into a ladder because I landed on that particular square on the board is just completely and utterly ridiculous." He gave his sore forehead a final rub. "Come on, let's get back to your place before the food gets cold."

He grabbed his bike by the handlebars and wheeled it to the curb. Sam was still standing there staring at him.

"Don't you think it's creepy?" Sam said. "I landed on a good-luck square, and I've had good luck all day. You landed on a bad-luck square with a ladder on it, and you've just bonked your head on a ladder." Sam's eyes narrowed. "Isn't that just a *little* weird?"

"No," Greg said, refusing to be drawn into Sam's little fantasy. "I think *you're* the one who's weird. Get your bike. I'm hungry."

"OK, have it your own way," Sam said, grabbing the handlebars with one hand and carrying the bag with the other. "But if I were you, I wouldn't go climbing any stepladders to wash windows tomorrow." He shook his head. "Absolutely no way!"

"Will you just shut up about it?" Greg said, losing his temper a little with his friend. "I am *never* going to believe that stupid game is giving us good luck and bad luck. It's complete garbage!"

He didn't believe for one moment that some old board game could have the power to influence a person's life. It was crazy. Impossible.

The next morning, when Greg and Sam and Mom and Edie arrived at Grandpa's house, Greg decided that perhaps he didn't feel like washing the windows after all.

"No problem," Sam said. "I'll do it."

He fetched the stepladder out of the cellar and got busy with a bucket and a cloth, cleaning the windows on the front porch.

Greg lugged a bunch of flat-packed boxes and some paper and tape up to the landing. He was going to get started on the bedroom.

He opened the door and carried the unmade boxes in and dumped them on the large double bed. He was just about to turn and get the reels of tape and the packing paper when he saw something that stopped him dead in his tracks.

The board game was out. Set up exactly the way it had been yesterday — with the blue figure and the red figure standing in the same places.

"What's going on here?" he murmured. "How did this get out again?" His eyes narrowed in alarm for a moment, then he gave a breath of laughter as he realized what must have happened.

"Oh, very funny, Sam!" he said. "You are such a comedian!"

Greg bounded down the stairs and ran down the hall. The front door was open, and the lower half of Sam was visible as he washed the higher panes of glass on the porch.

"Really funny," Greg said. "Ha-ha-ha. I ought to tip *you* off that ladder."

Sam doubled over and peered at him. "What are you talking about?"

"The game, dummy," Greg said. "Did you think I

was going to believe it had set itself up overnight? How stupid do you think I am?"

Sam looked at him. "Which question do you want me to answer first?" he said. He threw the cloth into the bucket.

"Oh, stop it," Greg said. "I *know* it was you. Who else could have done it?"

Sam frowned. "Are you trying to tell me that the game is out again?" he said.

"You know it is!" Greg replied pointedly.

Sam shook his head. "I didn't take it out."

"Oh, knock it off, Sam. It didn't scare me for an instant."

"I haven't even been up there!" Sam said with a hint of annoyance in his voice. "Besides, when would I have had the chance to do it?"

Greg stared at him. Sam had a point, now that he thought about it. There hadn't really been an opportunity for Sam to sneak away to the bedroom. It didn't make any sense.

Sam climbed down off the stepladder. "Show me," he said.

Greg led the way upstairs. The hairs were prickling

on the back of his neck, and his palms felt sweaty. He sensed something about all of this was not quite right.

As they entered the bedroom, Sam walked across the floor and stood over the open board, staring down at it. He was suddenly silent.

Greg heard a soft *swish* and looked around. The bedroom door had closed. There was the quiet click of the lock.

Sam turned to look at him, and the expression on his face was both angry and frightened. "I told you there was something weird about this game!" he said, his voice a low growl. "Look at what's happened!"

Greg walked over to the board. He could see right away that it had changed.

"That's not possible," he breathed, staring at the board in disbelief. A feeling of panic churned in his stomach.

The colored path still wound across the map, but now, most of the woodland that lay between the house and the town was gone, replaced by new buildings. And the town was different, too. There were more streets and more houses. And some of the old houses had been replaced by new ones.

Greg stared at their school. That hadn't been there before.

And the big parking garage had appeared as well.

So had the shopping center.

The map on the board still covered the same area — except it had been *updated* somehow.

Greg looked up at Sam. "How did this happen?" he whispered.

Sam didn't reply.

And then, Greg noticed something else that almost stopped his heart. The two figures that stood on the board had been repainted. The one on the ladder square had brown hair and was wearing a red shirt and black pants. The other one had blonde hair and was dressed in a white shirt and blue pants.

Greg stared up at his blonde-haired friend who was wearing a white shirt and blue jeans. He looked down at his own clothes.

Red T-shirt and black pants.

He fought desperately against the madness of it. He *knew* things like this couldn't happen. It had to be some kind of trick. A joke.

"No!" Greg gasped. "It's not real! It can't be real!"

"I'm going," Sam said, his voice thick in his throat. He turned, but as he did so, his shoe caught the cup that was standing unnoticed at his feet. The cup rolled over, and the dice spilled out.

They came up five.

Greg gave a hiss of fear as he saw Sam's piece quiver and shudder. Entirely unaided, it moved five squares forward on the board.

Greg scrambled away across the carpet, and Sam ran for the door. He grabbed the handle and twisted it, but the door remained closed. He struggled with the handle for a few moments. Then he turned his back to the door, staring across the room at the game, panting and wide-eyed.

"It's alive!" Sam shouted. "You have to make it stop!"

"I'll smash it up," Greg gasped. Slowly, reluctantly, he crawled across the carpet toward the board game. Up till then he had wanted to believe that someone was playing tricks on them, but there was no way of explaining away the fact that he had seen Sam's piece move on its own.

"Quickly!" Sam shouted, his voice filled with panic, still tugging at the door handle. "Before it does something else to us!"

Greg reached out and tried to flip the board closed. But it was as though it was glued to the carpet. He stretched his fingers toward his piece. Swallowing his fear, he closed his fist around it. A moment later, he fell back with a yell. It had been hot — too hot to touch. It had burned his hand.

While he was still recovering from the burning pain, he saw the rule book quivering on the carpet. The pages began to turn as though the booklet was caught in a fierce wind.

When the pages stopped fluttering, Greg felt a strange, horrible compulsion to crawl over to it and to see what the open pages showed.

In pale, faded handwriting he saw:

Vital Rules for Good Luck, Bad Luck
1. *Players MUST take their turn in the right order.*
2. *Players MUST finish the game.*

Greg turned to Sam. "We have to finish the game," he said, his voice a strained croak. "It says so . . . in the rules."

Sam shook his head. Greg could see that his friend

was terrified. Sam turned and struggled with the door handle again. The door didn't open. He thumped on the door with both fists. "Get me out of here!" he screamed at the closed door in frustration.

From downstairs, Greg could hear music on the radio in the kitchen. Edie was playing pop music at full volume, and it was loud enough to blot out any noise they might make.

"Don't you get it?" Greg shouted at Sam. "It won't let us out till we finish the game!"

"Mrs. Cranston!" Sam shouted, still beating at the door. "Help! Mrs. Cranston!"

Greg scrambled to his feet and ran over to his friend. He grabbed him by the shoulder. "It's pointless!" he said. "We have to finish the game."

"I'm not going near that thing," Sam said. Greg had never seen his friend like this.

"It's the only way," Greg said. "Listen to me!" He punched Sam's arm to get his attention. Sam stared at him, wild-eyed and panting. "Maybe we don't need to play the entire game," Greg said. "Maybe if one of us lands on a good-luck square we'll find a way to escape."

As he turned toward the game, a sudden thought struck him.

What kind of square had Sam's piece landed on after that last move? Good luck or bad luck?

A brown bird was drawn on Sam's square.

Greg sat back on his heels, puzzled. *A brown bird.* Was that good or bad? He stared at the rule book lying open on the carpet. He picked it up and went through it. Amazingly, there didn't seem to be any explanation of what the symbols meant.

Sam was still standing by the door, quiet now but still looking frightened.

"I can't figure it out," Greg said. "A bird could mean anything. I know one magpie means sorrow and two mean joy . . . but magpies are black and white. The bird here is brown — like a sparrow or something." He looked at Sam. "Do you know any superstitions that involve sparrows?"

Sam shook his head.

"No," Greg said. "Me, neither." He took a long, deep breath. "Oh, well — only one thing to do," he said. He picked up the cup and dropped the dice into it.

"Don't," Sam said.

Greg looked at him. "Relax!" he said, "I'm feeling lucky." It wasn't true, but he couldn't think of what else to say. They had to find a way of getting out of that room. They *had* to beat the game somehow. There would be plenty of time to go crazy thinking about exactly what was going on here afterward. He hoped.

He shook the cup and rolled the dice.

"Seven," he said. His heart thundered as he waited for his piece to move itself. But nothing happened. He let out a breath. "Well, at least that's an improvement," he said. He reached out cautiously. The piece was cool to his trembling fingertips. He paced out seven squares. He looked around at Sam. "It's one of those yellow squares."

"You need to take a card now," Sam said. He seemed to have calmed down a little. He walked slowly across the floor and stood beside Greg.

Greg lifted the top card off the deck and turned it over.

In that same faded handwriting, he read the words:

Survival Card: What's the Worst That Can Happen?
Better Keep Your Fingers Crossed!

"That's not so bad," Greg said. "What do you think it means?"

"I'm guessing it means cross your fingers and hope for the best," Sam said, squatting beside Greg and holding up both his hands. His fingers were already tightly crossed.

"Good idea," Greg said, crossing his own fingers. "It's your turn."

"I know," Sam said. He squatted there, staring at the board for several long, silent seconds.

"Well?" said Greg.

"OK, I'm just . . . you know . . ." Sam had a little trouble getting the dice back into the cup without uncrossing his fingers, but he managed it in the end. Then he picked up the cup between his two hands and shook it.

The dice spilled out.

Two sixes.

"Twelve," Greg said. "That's got to be good luck."

Sam pushed his piece along the board with the edge of his hand.

Greg peered at the square. It was dark blue with a bright yellow line zigzagging across it.

"I'm not sure what that's supposed to be," he said. "You look."

Sam leaned forward. His voice was low. "I think it's a streak of lightning," he said. He looked at Greg and there was fear in his friend's eyes. "Does that mean I'm going to be struck by lightning?" he breathed anxiously.

Greg looked out the window. "Not today. There isn't a cloud in the sky. And it probably won't happen at all if you do what the card says and keep your fingers crossed."

"That was *your* card," Sam said. "What makes you think it's going to help me?"

Before Greg got the chance to reply, his attention was taken by a curious fluttering noise. He looked around, trying to pinpoint the direction from which it was coming.

Sam was staring at the old fireplace. The hearth was empty except for an ornamental poker and a brass coal shovel. The fluttering sound became more frantic. It reminded Greg of the noise a flag makes when it's caught in a strong wind.

Sam stood up and moved toward the fireplace. "There's something —"

He got no further. A ragged shape suddenly burst out of the fireplace. It flew into Sam's face and then veered away at the last moment in a flurry of sooty wings.

Sam reeled back, his hands covering his face.

Greg clambered to his feet, watching the small shape as it circled the room. It was a sparrow. Somehow, it must have fallen into the chimney.

The bird made for the light of the windows. It got tangled for a moment in the net curtains, then managed to free itself and continue its wild circling of the room. It was in a total panic.

Greg ran over to the window, threw the net curtain aside, and tried to lift the sash, but it wouldn't budge. Seeing the bright light over his shoulder, the sparrow came careering toward the window. It crashed into the glass with a wild flapping of wings and then took off again — darting around the room in blind terror.

Sam ran at the bird as Greg watched in horror.

"I'll get you!" he shouted. Greg saw that Sam was

holding the poker from the fireplace, swinging it wildly at the bird.

"Sam! Stop!" Greg yelled.

"It's going to give me bad luck!" Sam shouted.

"Sam — you're crazy!" Greg called out. "Leave it alone! It can't hurt you!"

"No, I've got to stop it!" Sam shouted. "Otherwise something bad will happen!"

"It's just a harmless bird!" Greg screamed at his friend.

"The game sent it!" Sam screamed, swinging the poker wildly. "I have to get it!"

Exhausted, the bird came to rest for a moment on an old-fashioned brass wall light beside the bed.

"No!" Greg shouted.

But Sam wasn't listening. He was only a few feet away from the bird now. Greg could see its little chest rising and falling, its tiny eyes wide and alert.

Sam raised the poker above his head.

"Sam — be careful!" Greg shouted. "Watch out for the light!"

"I'll get you!" Sam yelled, lunging forward. He brought the poker down with a cry.

The sparrow was gone from the light fixture in a flash. But Sam couldn't stop the momentum of his blow. The poker crashed against the light fixture. One brass arm broke away and fell to the floor.

There was a dreadful hissing and spitting sound. Smoke burst from the light fixture in a blinding flash, and there were white and blue sparks everywhere. Greg ducked for cover as he suddenly realized what had happened.

His friend had gotten hurt.

As smoke filled the room, Greg crawled around in search of his friend and found him lying by the fireplace. Sam's hair was on end, his mouth was wide open, and his body was rigid. He was still clutching the poker.

"*Sam*, are you all right?" Greg gasped, almost choking with anxiety.

"Sam?" He shook his friend's shoulders. "*Sam!*" But there was no response.

Fighting for breath in the smoky room, Greg pulled himself away from Sam, who was lying on his side.

Suddenly, the bedroom door burst open. Greg's mother appeared in the doorway.

"The power is out," she shouted. "What on earth's happened?"

Greg stared at her. "Call an ambulance," he gasped, tears running down his face. "Sam's been hurt. It was the game! The game did it!"

Greg and his mother were sitting in the waiting area outside the hospital ward. It was evening, and they were waiting for the nurse to say they could go in and see Sam. Greg felt like they'd been waiting for days.

Greg's mother looked closely into his eyes.

"Are you feeling better now?" she asked.

Greg nodded.

She stroked his hair. "You had me worried for a while there," she said with a faint smile. "All that strange stuff you were saying about the game."

Greg gazed at her. He was shattered. All he wanted to do right then was to find a little hole somewhere, climb into it, and close it up behind him.

The memory of what had happened in the aftermath of Sam's accident was fuzzy in his brain. He knew he had been babbling about the game. He had told his mother that it was alive and out to get them. He had told her how the game wouldn't let them stop playing — how the board couldn't be moved.

After the paramedics had come and Sam had been taken away to the hospital, his mom had folded the board up without any trouble. Greg had noticed that the board no longer had the updated town on it. It looked the same way it did when they had first found it. His mother had put the pieces and the cards and the booklet back into the box and shut the lid. The two figures were back to normal. And the door must have unlocked itself.

A nurse approached Greg and his mother.

"You can go and see him until his parents arrive," she said. "He's still a little groggy, so you won't get much out of him."

"We just want to let him know we're thinking of him," said Greg's mother.

Sam was in a small side ward. There were four beds, and his was the only one occupied. Greg was startled by how small his friend looked in the hospital bed. Sam lay there, his face ashen and his arms resting on the covers. Both of his hands were heavily bandaged.

"Hello, Sam," Mrs. Cranston said gently, leaning over the bed. "How are you doing?"

He blinked up at her. "OK," he whispered.

"That's good," said Mrs. Cranston. "Tell you what — I'll leave you two alone to chat for a few minutes." She smiled down at him. "I'm glad you're feeling better, Sam."

"Thanks."

"I'll be just outside when you're ready," Mrs. Cranston said to Greg.

He nodded, watching her as she left the room. When he turned back to Sam, he saw fear in his friend's eyes.

"We didn't get to finish the game," Sam said.

"Yes, we did," Greg said gently. "Mom put it away."

Sam looked at him. "But is it going to stay where she put it?" he asked.

"It's just an old game," Greg said fiercely. "A stupid, old-fashioned, ordinary board game."

"Is that what you *really* believe?" Sam asked.

Greg gnawed his lower lip, avoiding Sam's eyes. "I don't know." If he refused to admit it out loud, maybe he could convince himself that the game wasn't really alive after all — that it wasn't really so terrible.

Sam raised his arms. "Look at what it did to me," he said. "You can't pretend it never happened."

Greg winced as he looked at his friend's bandaged hands. "I know," he said. He gave Sam a desperate look. "But maybe it's finished with us now."

"It should be smashed up or burned or something," Sam said quietly.

Greg looked at him. "I'm not going near it again," he said quietly. "Not ever."

Sam closed his eyes, saying nothing.

Greg stood there for a few moments, unable to think of a single thing to say to his injured friend.

The silence became uncomfortable.

"I think I'll go home now," Greg said at last.

"Fine," Sam said.

Greg looked anxiously at his friend. "I can't go back there," he said. "I can't."

Sam didn't respond.

"I'm really sorry you got hurt," Greg blurted. He walked quickly to the door and pushed through it.

He looked back at his friend as the door began to close.

A dart of anguish pierced his heart. Sam was sitting bolt upright in the bed. He was staring around the room as if he were still searching for the trapped bird — and there was a haunted, frightened look in his eyes.

I know you've had enough for one day," Mrs. Cranston said as they climbed into the car, "but I promised Mr. Shepherd at the nursing home that I'd drop by for a quick word with him this evening. Apparently your grandmother's been a little out of sorts the last couple of days." She glanced at him. "You don't mind, do you? It'll only take a few minutes."

"I don't mind," Greg said vaguely. He was still thinking about the expression he had seen on Sam's face as they left him. It had been very scary — and somehow *familiar*. And then it struck him. It was the same bewildered, distressed look that he had often seen on his grandma's face.

While his mother had a quick word with Mr. Shepherd, Greg found himself drawn to his grandma's room. If she was having a good day, he was going to ask her about that game. He had some very serious questions in need of answers.

He knocked and opened the door to her room. The TV was on — some game show or another. His grandmother was sitting up in a nest of pillows, staring vacantly at the screen, her weak old hands resting on the bedcovers.

She turned her head at the sound of him coming into the room, and her bleary eyes narrowed.

"Hi, Grandma. It's me, Greg."

She grimaced and made an incoherent noise in her throat.

"Grandma — it's OK. It's Greg."

She shifted uneasily in the bed, trying to focus on him.

"Get away!" she moaned. "You never give me any peace. Get away from me!"

She brought her arms up as if to protect her face. Her crippled hands flailed.

Greg took a step toward the bed and then froze.

He had never noticed before. He always avoided looking too closely at her twisted hands. But he noticed now.

Her fingers were crossed.

"Leave me alone!" she groaned. "I mean it! After all these years, can't you just leave me alone!"

Greg moved toward the bed. "Grandma! It's me!"

"No! No! No!"

Greg caught her thrashing arms. "Grandma! Stop it. I need to talk to you about the Good Luck, Bad Luck game. We found it in your armoire at the house."

Her eyes widened in terror, and she began to scream.

"Grandma! Please!"

But the old lady was wild with fear. Greg backed away from her. He had no idea how to cope with her in that state.

A nurse came running into the room. "What did you do?" she asked.

"Nothing," Greg gasped. "Nothing."

"Now, now, Lizzie, what's all this commotion?" The nurse reached for a buzzer on a cord that hung at the head of the bed. She looked at Greg. "I'll need help with her. Don't worry, we'll get her settled, but it's probably best if you leave us alone."

Confused, Greg backed out of the room. He closed

his eyes and leaned against the wall out in the hallway, taking long, heaving breaths like someone bursting up into the air out of deep, dark water. He was trembling all over. His legs felt so weak that he could hardly stand.

He was vaguely aware of people going into his grandmother's room. The shrill screaming died away, and a strange silence replaced it.

He opened his eyes, suddenly filled with a new determination. No matter how scary it would be, he knew what he had to do.

He ran down the hallway, passing the office where his mother was speaking with Mr. Shepherd. He ran down the stairs, across the reception area, and out through the front double doors.

Something had just fallen into place in his head. Neither he nor Sam had been able to figure out where the game ended on the old version of the board. It had been somewhere in town. And when the board updated itself, they had been so shocked that neither of them had thought to check it out. But now Greg knew exactly where that winding path of colored squares came to an end.

It ended at the nursing home. *The nursing home that had once been a lunatic asylum.*

He ran along the street, ignoring the curious glances of the people he sped past. He didn't hear the horns of the cars blaring as he ran heedlessly in front of them. He had only one idea burning in his mind: to get to his grandparents' house and destroy that game!

He ran across town and into the park. A cramp was biting into his side, but he ran on. Now he could see the chimney tops of the house among the trees.

He came to the wrought-iron gate and walked up the path. The front door was open a fraction of an inch. He assumed that the latch hadn't caught properly when they left the house.

Inside, the house was eerily quiet. As if it were holding its breath. Waiting for something.

Waiting for him?

He stood at the foot of the stairs. Gripping the banister, he could feel the hairs prickle on the back of his neck.

Slowly and determinedly, he made his way up the stairs.

From the landing, he could see that the bedroom

door was closed. The walls and the floor seemed to buckle and shift around him. Walking slowly along the hallway, he reached forward, turned the door handle, and pushed it open. He could feel his stomach turn when he realized the air still smelled of smoke.

For a moment or two, he didn't dare to look at that place on the carpet where the board had been set up.

What if it was there again?

He took a deep breath and turned his head.

He gasped.

The carpet was bare.

Still trembling a little, he walked over to the armoire. He was going to rip that board to pieces. Then he was going to smash the box and tear up the cards and the booklet. Then he'd break those two figures into small splinters.

And then the game wouldn't be able to hurt anyone ever again.

But the game wasn't in there.

He heard giggling coming from nearby.

He spun around. It was Edie's voice.

She must have come back here on her own.

"Edie?" he called, running to the door. *"Edie?"*

The door to another room along the hallway was slightly ajar. As he approached, he heard Edie's voice coming from inside the room.

"I found it!" she called. "I *knew* the two of you were doing something in there yesterday when you wouldn't let me in. You tried to hide it from me, but I came back and I found it!"

"Edie — what are you doing here?" Greg shouted. "What are you talking about?"

"I want us to play the game!" Edie shouted.

Greg stopped dead still. His whole body felt cold. He pushed the door wide open, already knowing what he would see, hoping desperately that he was wrong.

Edie was sitting cross-legged on the floor. The board game was set up in front of her. There were two figures standing on the board.

Edie had her fingers tightly crossed in her lap.

Greg stepped into the room and the door swung closed. "Edie, no . . ." he breathed.

"I already went," Edie said, grinning up at him. "It's your turn now."

GHOST IN THE MACHINE

"You're going to crash!" Rory McBride shouted to his sister. "Slow down or you won't make the bend!"

"Will you shut up! I know what I'm doing!" April yelled back.

The car took the curve at high speed. For a few moments, it really did look to Rory as if April might make it, but then the back wheels began to skid uncontrollably. A split second later, the front wheels hit the curb, and there was a kaleidoscope of movement through the windsield as the car left the road and tumbled over and over through the air. The scream of torn and smashed metal ended with a sickening thud as the car hit a wall and exploded.

There was a white flare, and red letters jumped on-to the screen:

YOU ARE SO DEAD! GAME OVER, ROOKIE!

"Rats!" April spat, dropping the controller into her lap. "I was going too fast."

"*Told* you so," said Rory with a grin. He was thirteen, a year older than his sister, and they both shared a passion for driving-simulation games.

"Move over," he said. "It's my turn."

April tossed her long black hair and narrowed her eyes in annoyance. Rory knew how badly she wanted to beat him. *In her dreams!* he thought.

"You think you drive better than me?" she said, raising an eyebrow. "I don't think so! You're just lucky."

"I'm a *totally* better driver than you," Rory said.

April's eyes glittered with the challenge. "If you say that boys make better drivers than girls, I'll clobber you. Got that?"

"Can't take the truth, eh?" laughed Rory, hitting the RELOAD button on the console.

"Well, for a start, Mom's a better driver than Dad," April said, poking him in the ribs with her toes.

"No way!" Rory replied, trying to fend off her attack.

"She is *so*," said April.

There was the sound of a car pulling up in front of the house. April ran to the window. "That should be her now. I'll go and ask her who the better driver is."

"Oh, right! Like Mom would admit that Dad's better," Rory replied.

"Oh, no!" gasped April, staring out the den window. "We'd better get outside, Rory."

"What's up?" Rory asked, his eyes still on the TV screen. But April left the room without replying.

Puzzled, Rory got up and looked out the window. There was something wrong with the family car. Black smoke was billowing out from under the hood. His mom was standing there, her hands planted on her hips.

Rory ran into the hallway and out through the front

door. April was already on the driveway, standing next to Mom.

"What's happened?" he said as a plume of black smoke rose slowly up over the car.

"Don't ask me," his mother replied. "It started doing this when I was in town. I barely managed to get it back here."

Rory heard feet on the stairs behind him. A moment later, his father was standing at his side, staring at the smoking car. "Elaine, what have you done?" he asked.

Oh, no, thought Rory. *That was definitely the wrong thing to say*.

"Excuse me?" Rory's mom said in a frosty tone.

"You've done it now, Dad," Rory whispered to his dad as his mom marched over toward them.

"What have *I* done, Michael? I'll tell you what *I've* done! I've made an executive decision about this horrible old wreck of a car. We're getting a new one, OK? One that's reliable, comfortable, and easy to drive. And this is *not* up for discussion."

Rory's mom had the same fierce gray eyes as April. When she unleashed one of the looks that Rory referred to as her "death stare," no one argued back.

"I'm not sure we can afford a new car right now," Mr. McBride began tentatively. "Maybe there's still some mileage left in this one. I'll take it to the mechanic tomorrow afternoon, and —"

Rory's mother pointed at the car. "I hate this machine," she said. "And it hates me. We hate each other! We are getting a new car, Michael."

"There's a huge new showroom on the other side of town," April added. "I saw something about it in the local paper. The ad said they have some great opening deals, and we can trade in this one."

Rory quickly chose to side with his mom. He really liked the idea of them getting a new, cooler car. "Come on, Dad! We could go and look around the showroom tomorrow. I'll help you choose!"

"Hey, me, too!" April added. "You can't rely on Rory, Dad. He'll just pick something flashy and fast. You're going to need sensible advice on all the extras, like a good stereo and a GPS and stuff like that."

"Well, it's decided," said Mrs. McBride, aiming one last disdainful look at the smoking car. "The two of you can go with your father to the showroom. I'm going to be stuck in the office tomorrow. There's a big all-day meeting with some clients from out of town, so I'm going to have to trust the three of you to pick the perfect car without me. Think *luxury*, Michael," she said, winking. "And listen to the kids!"

"Don't worry, Mom," Rory said. "We'll make sure Dad buys something good."

Admit it, Dad. You're lost, aren't you?" Rory asked, looking at his dad from the passenger seat. They'd finally gotten the car to work again, though Rory suspected that it was on its last legs.

"I'm *not* lost," his father replied. "I'm taking the scenic route, that's all."

Rory stared out at the gray warehouses that lined the street and sighed. "Dad, you are the *worst* navigator in the whole world. We should have gone back for the street map like I said from the start."

"I know where we're going, Rory," said his father testily. "It was that stupid detour that threw me off. How was I supposed to know they had suddenly decided to dig up the main street across town?"

"Which is exactly why you need a good GPS unit in the new car," April piped up. "That way, you can just tell it where you want to go, and it'll let you know the best way of getting there."

"Or I could remember to bring the street map," her father muttered, craning his neck to see what the holdup was.

"That didn't help you find the way to the motel at the shore last summer," April reminded him. "Mom said that you were driving in the wrong direction, but you didn't believe her *or* the road map!"

"And you got lost trying to find that big new shopping center out of town, remember?" Rory added with a grin. "And what about that time —"

"I get the picture," his father interrupted. "Your dopey dad can't find his way out of a paper bag. OK, I surrender — we'll get a GPS. Happy?"

"We could use a GPS unit right now," April mumbled. "We are *never* going to find the showroom."

Her father turned the car along another street. "Aha!" he said brightly. "I recognize this. Yes." He whooped with delight. "I know *exactly* where we are. The showroom is about five minutes away." The car sped up. "GPS!" their dad snorted. "Who needs it?"

———

Rory thought the car showroom was really impressive. It was located in a long, low, ultramodern building connected to a pristine lot where the vehicles were displayed. It had a massive stretch of reflective glass along the front, and long banners and trailing pennants displaying special opening offers and bargains.

A dozen or more shiny new cars stood on the lot under fluttering gold-and-silver banners. More expensive models were displayed on moving platforms inside.

Mr. McBride parked their car, and they got out. Rory saw several well dressed salespeople looking at them as they walked onto the lot.

"Hello, how may I help you?" asked one young man with an ultrasharp haircut and a smile like a camera flashbulb.

"We're just looking at the moment," replied Mr. McBride.

Rory grinned. He could see that his dad wasn't going to be rushed. But there were some amazing cars here. Picking one was going to be tricky.

They wound their way through the display models.

April wandered from car to car, and Rory peered in through the polished windows, drooling over the luxurious interiors and state-of-the-art technology.

"It's so hard to choose," April said, standing by a car with flame-red paintwork. "Can we have two, Dad?"

"Four would be better," Rory called after his father, who had moved on. "That's one each!"

"Just as soon as I win the lottery!" their father called back.

Rory spotted April hovering in front of a particular car. "Hey, Dad!" she yelled. "I've found one that Mom will go totally crazy about! Come and look."

Rory and his dad approached the car.

A saleslady came over to help. "It has all the features the discerning driver needs," she said. "ABS, onboard computer, cruise control, front and side air bags. It also has a multidisc CD player and driver and passenger climate controls."

"Does it have GPS?" April asked.

"That's an option," the saleslady said. "We have several different versions and we have trained mechanics on standby who can install the system of your choice within the hour."

Mr. McBride pursed his lips, staring at the price sticker on the windshield.

"Well —" he began, but Rory interrupted.

"We can afford it, can't we, Dad?" Rory said.

"Think how happy it would make Mom, not only to have a great car but for us not to get lost anymore!" April added.

"We can arrange very generous financing terms," the saleslady added quickly. "The paperwork won't take more than ten minutes." She smiled at April and Rory. "You could drive it away this afternoon! But I don't want to rush you. . . . Feel free to have a good look around. You won't find any better deals, I can promise you that."

"So?" April said. "Are we going to buy this wonderful, beautiful, fabulous car — or do you want to look at some others first, Dad?"

Her father looked at the car. "Do you think Mom will like it?" he asked.

"She'll love it!" Rory said. "It's awesome, Dad."

Mr. McBride walked around the car. "Well, let's take it for a drive," he said.

"And then can we buy it?" April said.

"We'll see," said her father.

"It'll drive like a dream," April said, smiling. "I just know it!"

Rory really enjoyed the test drive. April had been right: The car moved like a total dream, and the luxurious interior smelled of new leather and polish.

The saleslady got out of the front passenger seat and held the back door open for Rory and April to scramble out. She smiled at Mr. McBride over the car's shiny roof. "What did you think?" she asked.

"It's not a bad car," Mr. McBride replied, stroking his chin thoughtfully. "No, not bad at all."

"Give it up, Dad!" said Rory. "You know you *totally* love it!"

Their father looked at Rory and April and nodded. "OK," he said, smiling at the saleslady. "We'll take it!"

"And don't forget to get a GPS unit," Rory reminded him.

"A really good one," April added.

OK, kids," he said. "It's going to take them a little while to fit the GPS unit. How about we go and find somewhere to eat while we're waiting?"

"You made sure we got the best system, right, Dad?" April asked. "One of those talking ones that get their instructions straight from the satellite?"

"I didn't think we needed anything too complicated," said their father. "The one I bought was half the price of the high-end versions," he said. "But it has all the features we need. And the lady told me that there's a Web site where you can download new information as regularly as you need to. Apparently, the updated information can be loaded directly into the unit from a PC!"

April frowned at him. "The modern ones do that stuff automatically," she said.

"Yes, and they cost twice the amount of the one I got," their father replied. "It'll be great, you'll see. And by the way — since it was you two who insisted we needed the thing in the first place — I'm relying on you to figure out how to use it!"

Well, this is great," said Mr. McBride. "So much for your new technology!"

Rory peered out at the ROAD CLOSED sign directly ahead of them. Things had been going fine up until then. Rory had read the manual and had programmed their home address into the memory. At first, his dad seemed to be enjoying the new gadget, grinning every time the woman's pleasant mechanical voice gave them new instructions.

But his smile and cheery mood faded very quickly when they hit the construction work that had closed the main bridge over the river.

"So, how come the system didn't know about all this?" Mr. McBride asked. "Isn't that exactly the kind of thing it ought to warn us about? I'd be better off listening to the local radio station. At least they stay up-to-date." He poked at the controls on the dashboard.

"Don't panic, Dad," Rory said, pushing his father's hand aside and quickly finding the local news channel. "It'll work perfectly once we've downloaded the Web updates."

"It better work," grumbled his father, putting the car in reverse and maneuvering it onto the road that led alongside the river.

As they drove along, Rory looked back over his shoulder. He could see that the entire middle section of the bridge was missing. This was some major construction! Their only choice now was to go right around to the other bridge — a much longer route home. And to make matters worse, black clouds were gathering, and it was just beginning to rain.

"Fantastic!" groaned their dad. "Now the rain is going to ruin the wax finish before your mom even gets a chance to see it!"

"Look on the bright side," Rory said, pointing to the swishing windshield wipers. "The rain sensor made the wipers come on automatically."

"Hmm . . . well, I suppose that is something," his father said, leaning forward and pressing the OFF button on the GPS unit.

"*Good-bye,*" the robotic female voice said.

"And good-bye to you, too!" replied their father.

A jagged fork of lightning lit the sky for a moment.

"One . . . two . . . three . . . four . . ." Rory counted. A peal of thunder followed it. "That means the storm is just over four miles away," he said in his best scientist voice.

"It'll pass," his father said, having to speak loudly as the hammering of rain on the roof threatened to drown him out. "You'll see."

As they drove along, a second fork of lightning split open the sky for a second.

"One . . . two . . ." Thunder rumbled. "It's getting closer," Rory said. "It'll be right on top of us soon. And it sounds like it's going to be a really bad one!"

So? Do you like it?" Mr. McBride asked his wife. Rory, April, and their parents were standing in the shelter of the front porch. The new car was parked in the driveway for Mrs. McBride to look at.

"Like it?" said their mother. "I think so, but I can hardly see it!"

Rory gave a rueful smile. His mom was only exaggerating a little. The rain was now so heavy that the new car was hidden behind a veil of falling water that bounced high off the roof and hood and ran in rivers down the gray tarmac of the driveway.

She looked at April and Rory. "What do you both think?" she asked.

"We love it," Rory said.

"We could go for a ride in the rain," said their father. "Elaine? How about it?"

Their mother stared up at the heaving black clouds.

"Oh, why not?" she said with a smile. "I'm driving. You kids coming?"

"We've got to update the system!" Rory replied.

"He'll need my help, since I'm a better driver than Rory," April grinned, pushing her brother in the back.

"Go and get what you need from the car, and then we'll be off," their dad said.

Rory ran through the heavy rain, his T-shirt instantly sticking to his back. He took the GPS unit from its perch on the dashboard and grabbed the manual and PC connector cable from the glove compartment.

"Got it!" he shouted, running back toward the house, cradling everything under the front of his T-shirt to keep it dry. As soon as he got back into the doorway, April snatched the GPS unit and its accessories.

"I'll take those!" she said.

Mr. McBride lifted his coat up over his wife's head. "Ready? Set? Go!" he called, and Rory and April watched as their parents raced out into the pelting rain.

A huge jagged fork of lightning lit up the sky, and thunder boomed directly overhead. On the whole, Rory liked thunderstorms, but this one felt a little too close for comfort.

Rory waved, but his mom and dad didn't seem to notice. "Be careful!" he said, more to himself than anyone else. He watched the rain bouncing and bubbling on the path for a few more moments.

"I'm going in," April said. "It's freezing out here!"

"See you in a minute," replied Rory. He listened to the beating of the rain on the porch roof and the swirl of water in the gutters and drainpipes. It was good their house was on a hill. The way the rain was falling, some of the streets down by the river might actually get flooded. Rory stepped into the house and shut the door on the storm.

April was already in the computer room, seated at their PC, typing away. The monitor showed a colorful Web page, and April was entering information about the family.

"Did you find the Web site?" Rory said.

"Easily," April said. He could see that she had plugged the cable into the back of the navigation device and into a port on the PC.

"Do you want me to handle the download for you?" Rory asked.

April looked at him. "Not a chance!"

"Is it all plugged in right?"

"Of *course* it is." April flapped a hand at him. "Don't breathe down my neck."

"Don't mess it up." Rory grinned.

"I *won't*."

Rory watched as his sister located the Web page that allowed customers to download updated information. She clicked on the DOWNLOAD tab and leaned back triumphantly, her arms folded. "There — all done!"

"Mom and Dad aren't going to have much fun driving in this rain," Rory said, looking out the window. "I bet they don't go far. If it doesn't let up soon, we'll —" But the rest of what he had intended to say was lost as the sky suddenly exploded into a blinding blaze of white light, accompanied by a blast of thunder that seemed to beat the house like a drum.

There was an explosion, like the firing of a shotgun right above their heads — a terrifying, deafening sound that made Rory throw his hands over his ears and duck down. The loud bang filled the air, accompanied by another flare of blue-white light. April let out a scream as the lightbulbs overhead exploded.

Rory spun around and stared at the PC. Blue sparks

were pouring from the monitor, and there was a crackling, fizzing noise.

"April — get away from there!" Rory pulled his sister away from the computer table.

"What happened?" April yelled.

A tongue of flame licked over the blackened plastic casing, then they were plunged into absolute darkness. Rory could feel April clinging to him, her fingers digging into his arms. He could hear her harsh, panicky breath over the pounding of the blood in his temples.

"Rory — what was that?" she gasped.

"I'm pretty sure the house was struck by lightning," Rory said. "Are you OK?"

"I think so. The computer blew up right in my face."

"Are you hurt?"

"No. I'm fine. What happened to the lights?"

"I think the lightning must have wrecked all the wiring in the house," Rory said. "Wow!" He looked at his sister and managed to make a grin. "We're lucky we weren't fried." He clambered to his feet and looked out the window. The streetlights were still on outside — and other houses glowed with light through the rain. "It seems to have been just our house that got hit," he said. "I've got a flashlight in my room. Stay here, and I'll go and get it."

"I'm coming with you," April said as she got shakily to her feet. "I'm not staying here all alone. The PC might burst into flames or something."

"I suppose we should get the fire extinguisher from the cellar," Rory said. "Just to be on the safe side." He carefully felt his way toward the door, circling the room to avoid going too close to the computer table. There was a nasty smell of melted plastic, and acrid smoke floated in the air.

They found a flashlight and made their way downstairs into the cellar. It was rather creepy to be down there without the lights on. Sinister black shadows loomed all around them, and the smell of burned plastic was very strong.

Rory shined his flashlight on the main circuit box at the far end. "April — look at this," he breathed, his voice shaking. The box was melted. Wisps of gray smoke were filtering up from it. He peered at the blackened and misshapen box. "It's a total mess," he said.

"Do you think it's safe?" April asked. "Could it catch fire?"

"I don't know." Rory was reluctant to get any closer. "Let's just grab the fire extinguisher and get out of here." He looked at her. "We ought to check around the house really fast. If the computer blew up, then other electrical stuff might have done the same."

They headed back to the stairs. Rory unclipped the small red fire extinguisher from the wall.

Rory led them in a quick check of all the downstairs rooms. Everything was in darkness, but there was no telltale smell of burned plastic. It was beginning to look like the computer had taken the full force of the lightning strike.

They went back up to the computer room. Rory pointed the flashlight at the computer. The monitor's flat-screen LCD panel had melted completely, and Rory could feel sticky pools of melted plastic crunching and squishing under his feet. One side of the computer was blackened and burned away, but there was no sign that it might still be on fire.

"I think it's safe," he said.

"It doesn't look too safe to me," April said.

"I meant it doesn't look like it's going to catch fire," Rory said. Then he remembered something that made the whole lightning strike even worse. "The GPS unit! It was plugged in. . . . It'll be a goner for sure."

"Oh, *no*," April groaned.

Rory traced a cable from the back of the charred PC. Its other end was still plugged into the small navigation unit that was sitting on the edge of the table.

He moved the flashlight closer — hardly able to believe his eyes. The device seemed untouched by the lightning strike. "Hey, it looks OK," he said.

April leaned close. "That's amazing! Is it still working?"

Rory pressed the ON button. To his astonishment, the screen light came on, and the words DOWNLOAD COMPLETE appeared in large black letters.

"Awesome!" April said.

"It's completely OK," Rory said. "Unbelievable!"

"Let's get out of here," April said. "We'll get some help from next door till Mom and Dad get home."

Rory nodded. They went downstairs, and he put the navigation unit on the hall stand. They had only gone a few steps when they saw the headlights of a car approaching.

"It's Mom and Dad!" Rory said in relief.

The car turned and glided into their driveway.

His mother's window slid down and she stared at him in surprise. "What's going on?" she asked. "Why are all the lights out?"

Rory helped his dad go around the house and unplug all the electrical items. Mr. McBride gave a long, low whistle when he saw the damage to the computer. "The lightning bolt must have been a direct hit," he said, shaking his head. "It's strange that nothing else appears to have been affected." He shook his head. "I don't know," he added, looking at Rory. "We leave you two alone for ten minutes, and you manage to get the house struck by lightning." He gave a lopsided, disbelieving smile. "Typical."

"It wasn't funny, Dad!" Rory said. "We could have been blown to bits."

"No," his father said, his face suddenly serious again. "I'm sure it wasn't remotely funny." He reached out and patted Rory's shoulder. "But look on the bright side:

No one was hurt — and we're having an adventure in the dark."

There was the sound of the front door opening and closing.

"That should be April and your mom with dinner," his father said. Sure enough, a few moments later, the two of them came into the room, accompanied by thick paper cartons and the smell of Chinese food.

After the meal, Mrs. McBride took all the ice cream out of the freezer. "No point in letting it defrost and go bad," she said, handing out spoons.

She had made the house feel really cozy, lighting plenty of candles in the kitchen and the den and some more in carefully chosen places in the hallway and on the upper landing.

Maybe the power being out isn't such a bad thing, Rory thought as he scooped out another spoonful of chocolate chip ice cream. *Like Dad said — it's an adventure.*

Just then, something caught Rory's eye. "That's odd," he said aloud. The green timer light on the microwave was flashing on and off. "I'm *sure* it wasn't doing that before." When he and his dad had checked the house, there had been no sign of anything electrical working.

The timer showed four zeros — slowly blinking on and off. It looked a little eerie in the candlelight. Mrs. McBride went over to it and pressed some buttons, but the flashing row of zeros didn't change.

"It's definitely not working," she said.

"That makes sense," said Mr. McBride. "I unplugged it."

"So why's the light still on?" Rory asked.

"Some sort of internal battery, I suppose," said his father. "Lots of household devices have emergency batteries to keep the clocks running when the power is off."

"So why is it just showing zeros?" April asked.

"Beats me," her father said. "So . . . who's up for a game of Clue by candlelight?"

Everyone headed for the living room. Rory was the last out, and as he left, he glanced over his shoulder. He froze. For an instant, the flashing display had looked different.

Instead of the four zeros, he could have sworn he saw the word RO:RY.

He blinked. This time the clock read four zeros again.

"Hey, come on, slowpoke!" April called from the living room. "There's a murder to be solved in here!"

Feeling a little unsettled, Rory headed for the den.

That night, Rory lay in bed with his hands folded behind his head, staring up into the darkness. He had never even considered before how many totally ordinary things he used every day were dependent on electricity.

With the power out, the family had been reduced to sitting on the living-room carpet playing Clue in a ring of small candles. Once they'd finished the game, he couldn't even zone out in front of the TV or listen to his music. And candlelight might look nice, but he and April were *way* too old for the ghost stories that their dad was desperate to tell them.

He turned over in bed and pulled the covers over his ears. Hopefully, the emergency electrician would be there first thing in the morning, and then they'd be able to get back to normal. But sleep felt a long way off. He lay tossing and turning, unable to get comfortable.

In the darkness behind his closed eyelids he could still see the microwave's green display panel.

00:00. RO:RY. 00:00.

He sat up, forcing his eyes open — forcing the image out of his head.

"It wasn't real!" he whispered aloud to himself. "I imagined it." He lay back, eyes wide, determined to forget the disturbing image.

He let his eyes close.

The eerie green lights came floating back.

Eventually, he drifted off into troubled sleep, but the flashing display was with him all night.

The electrician lifted his baseball cap and scratched at his closely shaven head. "That must have been some lightning strike," he said, illuminating the damaged fuse box with the light of a large, square flashlight. "I've never seen anything like this before. The fuses are melted together."

It was about ten o'clock the next morning. Mr.

McBride was with the electrician down in the cellar. Rory and April were perched on the steps, listening to what the man had to say.

"Can you fix it?" April asked.

"It'll take a while," he said. "But I'll get the power back on for you, don't worry." He stared at the melted box. "What I can't figure out is why the water pipes and the copper in the electrical circuitry didn't ground the strike. Nothing should have blown up. You should have been perfectly fine. I don't understand it. I'll just go and get my gear from the van, and then I'll get to work."

"Is it OK if I watch?" Rory asked.

"Don't be a nuisance, Rory," said his father.

"That's not a problem," said the electrician. "I don't mind an audience. And he can hold the flashlight for me."

Both April and Rory hung around to share duties in holding the powerful flashlight and bringing the electrician cold drinks and cookies.

It was almost noon before he finally replaced and rewired the main fuse box.

"Switch on the light, Rory," he said. Rory reached up and flicked the light switch for the cellar. Nothing happened.

"Uh-oh," Rory said.

The electrician laughed. "April, come here, will you? You can do the honors."

April stood next to him.

"See the red lever?" he said. "Pull it down for me."

"I won't get blown up, will I?" she asked.

"No, I promise you won't get blown up," the electrician said.

April flipped the lever on the side of the new fuse box.

All three of the bulbs in the cellar went on. "And that's magic!" the electrician said.

"Will everything be OK now?" Rory asked.

"I don't see why not," said the electrician, gathering his tools.

"The computer won't be," said April glumly. "It's totally wrecked."

After the electrician had left, April and Rory ran into the den and put on their favorite music channel on TV.

"That's the last of the peace and quiet, I suppose," said Dad, sitting down with his newspaper.

"So when will we get the new computer, Dad?" April asked.

"Can we help choose it?" Rory added. "There's this great flat-screen one that my friend Matt's got —"

"Stop right there, Rory," his dad said. "That won't be an issue till we get the insurance money. I've called them and filed the claim, but I'm afraid you might have to do without a computer for a few weeks."

Rory and April looked at each other. No computer. That was *very* bad news.

How long till dinner, Mom?" Rory asked, sticking his head around the kitchen door.

"It'll be next week at this rate," exclaimed his mother. Rory could see that she was looking stressed.

"What's wrong?" he asked.

"It's this stupid oven," she said. "That lightning strike must have done something to it. I can't get it to behave. Either it doesn't heat up at all, or it heats up too much! I've been trying to get it to work correctly for more than an hour now."

Rory walked across the kitchen and twisted the control knob for the oven.

"Don't!" his mother said, snatching his hand away.

"I was just trying to — oh!" The rest of what he had intended to say was drowned out by a loud fizzling sound — as if a big firework had been set off inside the oven. Then there was a hollow bang, and black smoke began to filter out of the closed oven door.

Rory gave his mother an anxious look. "Oops," he said. "Sorry."

Mrs. McBride opened the oven door. A moment later, the smoke alarm on the ceiling began to emit a piercing beeping noise.

"Switch that thing off," Rory's mom shouted. "And I'll open some windows."

Rory grabbed a broom and used the handle to press the RESET button.

Rory's father appeared in the doorway. "Problem?" he asked.

"You'd better . . ." Mom began.

". . . order pizza," Mr. McBride said, making a hasty retreat.

133

Rory's mother sat at the kitchen table with her head in her hands. "This is all such a pain, Rory."

Rory stood at her side. "It'll be OK, Mom," he said, patting her shoulder. "Dad said the insurance should cover anything that's gone kablooey." He picked up the place mat from the table and waved the smoke away. "And it doesn't seem like anything else is messed up."

As if in response to his words, a dull metallic rumble began to sound from the other side of the kitchen.

They both turned to look.

The washing machine had started — with nothing in it. The red lights on the control panel were lighting up — blinking on and off at random as the empty barrel turned.

Rory quickly walked across the room and flipped the switch on the wall socket to the OFF position. The washing machine continued to rumble away.

"How's it doing that?" he asked, staring at the switch on the socket. He flipped it back and forth several times, but still the machine churned away under the work surface.

A few moments later, his mother's arm reached out

past him and pulled the plug. The machine came to a sudden stop.

They looked at each other.

Rory was baffled. "It was still working after I turned the power off," he said.

"There must have been some energy left in the power cord," his mother replied, her voice tight and strained.

He looked over his shoulder at the silent washing machine. "But that *can't* be right," he murmured. "Either the power's on, or it isn't."

"Well, I'm in the mood for pepperoni," she said with forced brightness. "How about you, Rory?"

Rory stared at her.

She was trying to pretend it hadn't happened — except it *had*. Electricity simply couldn't behave like that. It was impossible. Rory had the creepy feeling that things were beginning to get out of control.

He wondered what was going to happen next.

Rory was awoken from a deep sleep that night by a piercing electronic shriek. At first, he thought it was the smoke alarm again, but it was coming from close by.

He turned his head to look at his digital alarm clock. His eyes were still bleary from sleep, but he could clearly see the display flashing in the darkness of his room.

00:00

11:11

22:22

It was changing rapidly. In the stillness, the noise felt as if it were boring into his brain.

"Shut up!" he mumbled, slamming his hand down on the STOP button. The noise stopped, but it left a weird ringing in his ears. "Stupid thing," he grumbled, turning over and pulling the covers up over his ears.

Seconds later, the alarm's radio began to blare out. It was a foreign voice — a man talking excitedly. Annoyed, Rory threw back the duvet and switched on the bedside light. He pulled the radio alarm clock into his lap and rolled down the volume control until the voice was just a whisper.

As he lay back down, a thought struck him. He *always* kept the radio tuned to a music station. Changing it could have been a dumb joke of April's, but it didn't seem to be her style. Rory sat bolt upright and picked up the clock again. The digital display began to change more rapidly, speeding up until the red numbers were just a blur. It began to feel hot in Rory's hands.

Panicked, he dropped it onto the duvet, bunching himself up in a corner of the bed, watching the whirling numbers.

Gradually, the blur slowed.

The numbers came to a halt.

But they weren't numbers anymore.

The display matched the display on the microwave before: RO:RY.

Rory stared at the red letters, his heart pounding and a cold feeling growing in his stomach. *Not real. No way!* He closed his eyes and opened them again.

Now the fiery letters spelled out something else — something that brought Rory's heart up into his throat and made him gasp for breath.

The display read: SO:ON.

Trembling violently, Rory reached toward the clock. A crackle of blue sparks jumped from the machine to his fingertips — stinging him, making him cry out in pain. He clutched his hand to his body, frozen in absolute panic.

Staring down at the display, Rory desperately hoped that the whole thing was a figment of his imagination.

03:15

A quarter past three in the morning.

Rory let out a gasp of breath. The nightmare was over, but he was still shaking. He gave himself a few seconds to recover from the bizarre ordeal.

This is so weird, he thought. *What was that?*

He climbed out of bed and reached for the plug. He pulled it clear from the wall, and the display went out.

"I don't know if what just happened was real or not," he murmured. "But I'm not taking any chances."

He picked up the dead alarm clock and wrapped the cord around it.

"You're going somewhere where you can't give me any more creepy messages, OK?" he said. He shivered slightly as he recalled first seeing the message on the front of the microwave the day before.

Were these things trying to tell him something?

But that's impossible, right? Rory's mind raced. He shook his head to clear it. Rory wasn't going to let thoughts like *that* into his head in the middle of the night. No way.

Bundling the alarm clock up in a sweatshirt, Rory stuffed it in the bottom drawer of his night table and got back into bed.

The display *couldn't* really have spelled out his name. It *couldn't* have made words. That must have been his imagination working overtime.

But it was a long time before he managed to get back to sleep.

Rory padded into the kitchen, the tiles cold against his bare feet. It was early the next morning, and he had not slept well after the incident with the alarm clock.

He stepped into icy-cold water.

He gave a startled yelp and stared down. A wide pool of water was spreading across the floor from the fridge.

"What are you yelling about?"

Rory looked around. April was standing in the kitchen doorway.

"There's cold water all over the floor," Rory said. "I think the fridge is busted."

Their mother came up behind April. "Oh, good grief," she groaned, staring at the slippery floor. "Is this ever going to end?"

April was sent to fetch towels, and the family mopped up the water and wrung it out into the sink while Mr. McBride checked out the fridge.

He gave them a look. "You're not going to believe this," he said, opening the freezer compartment door, "but it's actually hot inside here. The thing has gone haywire. We'll have to throw everything out."

Mrs. McBride sniffed the milk carton. "Urgh — it's gone bad," she said. "Rory, head down to the store and get us some milk, please."

"And some orange juice," April added.

"And you'd better get some butter, too," said Mr. McBride, handing Rory some money.

By the time Rory got back with the provisions, the table was set for breakfast.

It was an unsatisfying, miserable meal — just cereal and cold drinks and long faces all around.

"When are we going to get the electricity working again?" April asked grumpily. She liked butter on toast for breakfast, but the toaster wasn't working.

Rory's dad got up and walked into the den. After a couple of minutes, he came back and sat down.

"I've called the electrician. He's all booked up today. The earliest he'll be able to come over is first thing tomorrow."

"Can we watch TV?" April asked hopefully.

"I don't think we should use anything electrical," said her father. "Just to be on the safe side."

"*No TV?*" April gasped. "That's it! I'm out of here." She got up from the table and headed for the hallway. "I'm going to spend the day at Rachel's."

"I want you back here by five," Mom insisted. "You've got homework to do before school on Monday. Don't forget that your father and I are playing cards at the Tannenbaums' this evening."

"Yes . . . great . . . fine . . . *wonderful!*" April shouted as she stomped her way upstairs.

The Tannenbaums. Rory groaned to himself at the very thought of them. They were the *most* boring of all his mom and dad's friends. When the four of them got together, they'd just sit playing cards for hours on end. *At least it's not Mom and Dad's turn to have them over*, he thought with some relief.

A minute or so later, April came back into the kitchen. She was fiddling with her MP3 player and frowning. "All my music's disappeared!" she said. She threw the gadget on the table. "Is every single thing in this house useless now?" She glared at her father. "Do you know how long it took me to download all my favorite tracks?"

"Can't you download them again from Rachel's PC?" Rory suggested. "She's got the same MP3 player as you."

"I *suppose* so, seeing that I don't have any other choice," April said crossly. "Is it OK if I go over there now?"

Mrs. McBride looked at her watch. "It's only nine o'clock," she said. "Isn't it a little early?"

"Rachel's mom won't mind," April said, heading for the door. "Besides, there's nothing to do around here anyway."

"Homework?" her father tried.

"Housework?" Mom suggested, smiling.

"Nice try!" April said, laughing as she ran out of the kitchen.

The day wasn't as boring as Rory had feared. Despite the fact that all his friends had other things to do, he managed to keep himself happily occupied.

He passed a couple of hours helping his dad in the yard, pruning the hedges and pulling out the weeds from the flower beds. Then he disappeared up to his room to read a few of the comics that had stacked up over the past couple of weeks while he'd been too busy with his new driving simulation game. When his mother popped her head around his bedroom door to tell him she was going to order Mexican for dinner, he was surprised at how the time had flown by.

"OK, Rory," Mrs. McBride said as she cleared up after dinner. "We'll only be a few blocks away. The Tannenbaums' phone number is on a Post-it note on the fridge door. If you need us, just call. And if it's really urgent, you're to go next door. Got that?"

"Yes, Mom," Rory said. The next moment, he heard the front door open.

"I'm back!" April said, wandering into the kitchen.

"If you get hungry later, there are some snacks in the cabinet," their mother told them. "And once you've finished your homework, there are plenty of board games to keep you busy."

"I'm going to wash my hair," April announced. "At

143

least the hot water runs on gas. Can you imagine if we couldn't even take showers? Yuck!"

After his mom and dad had gone and April was in the bathroom, Rory draped himself over the sofa and went back to his comics. There would be plenty of daylight to read by for another hour or so, and he was sure that his parents wouldn't be back that late.

About half an hour had gone by when his concentration was disturbed by a faint buzzing sound. He looked up, turning his head to identify the sound. It was familiar, but he couldn't place it.

After listening to the buzzing for a minute or so, he got up and opened the door into the hall. The noise grew louder. It was coming from upstairs.

Suddenly, Rory realized exactly what it was that he was listening to.

It was a hair dryer.

"April!" he gasped, racing up the stairs. She had been told not to use *anything* electrical!

Rory pushed his sister's bedroom door open. "April?" he called uneasily.

"Help me!" April croaked in a hoarse, fractured voice. She was doubled over, struggling with the hair dryer. Rory felt terror grip him as he saw that a huge chunk of her wet hair was caught up in the dryer. The motor of the machine was growling and roaring, and the hair dryer's cord was somehow wound around his sister's neck.

Rory lunged forward, desperate to help. At that moment, she fell onto her side on the floor, clawing helplessly at the cord around her neck.

"It's attacking me," she managed to force out, and Rory watched her face turn more and more red.

"Hold on!" Rory shouted, and he dropped to his knees, snatching at the dryer. Tentacles of smoke were rising up from April's scorching hair, and Rory's eyes began to stream from the thick, pungent smoke. He managed to get his fingers between April's neck and the hair dryer cord, but it seemed to twist and get tighter. All the while, it roared hysterically, as if it were filled with hostile life.

Rory could feel his heart pounding in his chest. His sister's face was going blue. He ran over to the wall and pulled the plug out of the socket.

The hair dryer went silent and crashed to the carpet like a dead thing.

April pulled the cord loose and curled up on the floor, her knees up to her chest, coughing and choking.

Rory found scissors on his sister's dressing table and cut her hair to free her from the dryer. "April?" He shook her. "April! Are you all right? What happened?" He pulled her up into a sitting position. There was a nasty red welt around her neck.

"I plugged it in," April gasped. "But the cord was all tangled up, and while I was trying to get the knots out, the thing turned on all by itself." She stared wide-eyed at him. "I tried to drop it, but it was like it was alive. It pulled itself right out of my hands!" She gulped. "It went around my neck, and then my hair got sucked in." She shuddered. "It was so scary."

"You're OK now," Rory said. "Can you get up?"

"Yes . . . I think . . . so," she replied.

"There's something really wrong with the house," Rory said. "We have to get out."

April nodded. Rory helped her to her feet. "Rory? What's happening?"

"I don't know," Rory said, holding her steady. He stared into her frightened eyes. "I don't think the lightning that hit us was *normal*. I think it's done something to the whole house."

He helped April out onto the landing. From downstairs, he could hear loud music playing. It was the powerful system in the living room — blaring out music at full volume.

Rory looked at his sister. "The stereo isn't plugged in," he said.

"It *must* be," April said, staring down the stairwell. "How could it do that if it's not plugged in?"

He looked at his sister and could see the growing terror in her face. "We'll be OK," he said, trying to sound as if he really believed it. "I'll get us out of here. Don't worry."

More noise rang out from the TV room. Loud, distorted voices. The television burst into life, flickering through the channels — one after another, faster and faster.

"Come on," Rory said, grabbing her hand. "We'll go straight for the front door, OK?"

Hand in hand, they raced down the stairs.

April looked over her shoulder. "What's that?" There was more noise — coming from the kitchen.

"Don't think about it," Rory said. "Run!"

Behind them, he could hear the rumble of the washing machine, and other whirring and grinding noises — as if every electrical appliance in there had somehow burst into life, angry at them for trying to leave.

Rory ran for the front door, pulling his sister along behind him.

He reached for the lock, but as he did, April shouted a warning.

"Rory! Look out!" she called.

There was a snapping sound as the cable that ran up the wall alongside the door pulled itself out of its staples and wrapped itself around the handle. As Rory stared in disbelief, the broken end whipped out toward him, lashing across his cheek.

Rory fell back with a yell of pain.

Blue sparks spat out from the lock. Rory gasped as the end of the cable snapped in the air like a whip.

"Get away from it!" April shouted. "We can use the back door!"

Rory knew that meant going through the kitchen with all its roaring and bellowing electrical devices, but surely that had to be better than the snakelike cables piercing the air.

"Yes! Go!" he gasped.

They ran for the kitchen, but the way to the back door was blocked by what looked like a spiderweb of wires stretched across their path.

"What are we going to do!" screamed April over the tumult.

Rory had no idea. The radio and the portable TV set were howling. The coffee grinder was whining at full speed. The blender blades were whirring. The food processor was grinding away. Behind those sounds was the steady growl of the washing machine and the shriek of the dishwasher.

Then Rory saw the digital display on the microwave. It was flashing rapidly.

RO:RY

SO:ON

RO:RY

SO:ON

"R-Rory?" April stared at the flickering display, and she began to scream.

Rory grabbed her and pulled her back out of the

doorway as a fizzing wire came lashing toward them. He slammed the door, hearing the fierce *thwack* of the wire on the wooden door panels.

"April — stop screaming and think!" Rory shouted, dragging his sister's hands away from her face.

She stared at him, silent now, but panting with fear. "We can still get out through the garage."

The internal door to the garage was in a small utility room that led off the hallway. Rory opened the door to the room. It was filled with shelving units stacked with his father's gardening equipment.

Rory took April's hand and pulled her into the room. They were probably safe; he was pretty sure there wasn't anything electrical to attack them. He ran for the garage door and wrenched it open. There was a sudden surge in the noise from the rest of the house, bearing down on them from all sides, rising like an electronic chorus of rage.

The ceiling light burst on and off, and the bulb exploded over their heads, spraying them with tiny shards of glass.

Rory and April ran through the door and slammed it shut behind them.

"What do we do now?" April gasped.

Rory ran alongside the car to the large metal garage door. It was the type that lifted up into the ceiling. He hammered the heel of his hand against the button that should open the door. There was a brief crunch of gears, but the door didn't move.

"Rory! Watch out!" April's voice was shrill with panic. A moment later, Rory threw himself backward as a pair of thick wires wrenched themselves free of the wall and lunged toward him.

The fluorescent lights on the ceiling came on with a fizzing noise. Sparks showered down.

"Rory!" April shouted. "What're we going to do now?"

"In the car," Rory replied. "We'll be safe in there." The car hadn't been anywhere near the house when the lightning had struck. It had to be a safe refuge.

His father had reversed the car into the garage to make for an easy start in the morning, so the front of the car was facing the big metal door. Rory opened the driver's door, and the two of them hurtled themselves into the car. Rory slammed the door closed. April scrambled into the passenger seat, gasping for breath, her wide, frightened eyes staring out through the windshield.

"We'll sit here and wait till Mom and Dad get home," Rory said calmly. "They'll know what to do."

April looked at him. "I'm not sure the car will protect us for that long," she said. "We might need to find our own way out."

Rory gave a tight smile, desperate to reassure his sister. "I'll think of something," he said. He felt for the spare key under the seat.

As he found it and breathed a sigh of relief, there was a roaring and a clattering sound from the back corner of the garage. Rory twisted in his seat and peered through the rear window. He saw something rise up from under a plastic sheet. There was a grinding, rattling snarl as the thing lifted into the air.

"Oh, no," Rory groaned. In an instant, he remembered what his dad kept back there.

"Rory," April said, clutching his arm. "What is it?"

"The hedge trimmer," Rory said, cold sweat beading on his forehead.

The sheet finally slipped away, and the grinding,

vibrating blades of the hedge trimmer were revealed. It stopped for a few moments, as if seeking out prey, then the long blade turned toward them.

The hedge trimmer smashed through the back window of the car, shattering it into a maze of pieces. The blade drew back and lunged again. Fragments of glass ricocheted around the inside of the car, but Rory saw that the wire was tangled up in something outside. The howling and clanking blade could not reach them.

"Rory!" April shouted. "We have to get out of here, otherwise we'll be killed! You'll have to start the car!"

Rory stared at his sister. He had never been behind the wheel of a *real* car. But he knew that April was right. At any moment, the tangled wire of the hedge trimmer could free itself — and then it would come crashing right through and puncture the front seats.

He pushed the key into the ignition and turned it.

The engine came alive immediately. *Thank goodness*, Rory told himself. The new car was an automatic. He tried to remember each step his parents performed when either of them was in the driver's seat.

His brain was in a whirl, but somehow he kept calm enough to get the car rolling forward. The hedge trimmer slipped out of the back window and fell to the ground, but he could still hear a dreadful noise as it thrashed on the concrete. Swallowing a lump in his throat, he stamped down hard on the accelerator. The car leaped forward with a jerk and banged into the large metal garage door with bone-shaking impact.

Rory winced as he saw the buckled and dented hood of the car. The door was dented, too, but it hadn't moved. The wires slapped against the car's windows.

"You have to hit it harder!" April shouted to him. "Go faster!"

Rory managed to get the car into reverse. It lurched backward into the garage, catching the body of the hedge trimmer under the rear bumper and dragging it along the floor. The bladed machine's motor screamed in frustration. The car banged hard against the back wall before he could stop it. Summoning all his courage, Rory put the car into drive and slammed his foot down on the accelerator.

The car lunged forward, and Rory gritted his teeth as they hurtled toward the garage door.

There was a crash and crack of metal.

"You did it!" April said excitedly.

Rory watched as the door crumpled and the car made it through.

He looked at his sister. April's eyes were wide. "You saved us!" she gasped.

"I did, didn't I?" Rory breathed, bringing the car to a halt on the driveway. He looked over his shoulder. The lights in the house were flashing rapidly on and off. It was as though the entire place was tearing itself to pieces in rage at their escape. Rory could see that neighbors were beginning to trickle out of surrounding houses, staring.

But they were safe now. "Maybe we should walk from here . . ." he said, giving April a weak smile.

"I think that would be a *very* good idea," April replied. She pushed at the door handle to get out. The door didn't move. "It's stuck," she said. "We'll have to get out your side."

Rory turned the keys and pulled them out of the ignition, but the low, steady purr of the engine didn't stop. *That's weird*, he thought to himself. He reached for the handle of his own door. As he did so, the central-locking button snapped downward. "What is —" Rory was cut off by something that filled him with renewed dread.

The GPS unit was back in its place on the dashboard.

And it was on.

April was staring at the brightly lit screen. "Rory," she said, her voice low and trembling. "Did you do that?"

"It wasn't me," Rory replied, his voice barely above a whisper. "I didn't even know it was in here. Dad must have put it back."

"Why has it turned on?" April asked.

Rory swallowed hard. "I don't know," he said.

Before April could reply, a mechanical voice spoke. It wasn't the friendly female voice that they had heard before. It was a low, guttural, rasping voice that sent chills up Rory's spine.

"You wish to go to Dunbar Street," it grated.

April looked at Rory. "The voice . . . .it's changed," she said shakily.

The voice croaked again. *"From Howard Lane you must turn left onto Orchard Avenue."*

"Why is it telling us that?" April asked, her voice trembling.

"We have to get out of the car!" Rory shouted. "Now!"

He fought desperately with the handle. The hideous voice spoke again, fiercer and more insistent now. *"You must turn left onto Orchard Avenue!"* it snarled.

Rory twisted in his seat and kicked at the door. In a moment, the car was backing up toward the garage.

"It's taking us back into the garage!" April screamed.

Suddenly, the car halted. The engine revved wildly, and Rory watched as the gear shift flicked into drive and the accelerator pedal slammed down to the floor. The car leaped forward, pinning them in their seats. It crashed down the driveway and bounced down onto the street. The steering wheel spun. April and Rory were thrown to one side as the car careered along the street.

Rory grabbed the steering wheel in both hands, stomping down on the brake pedal. But the wheel spun in his grip, wrenching at his arms. And the brake pedal was useless. . . .

The car began to gather speed, and April let out a scream as they narrowly avoided a head-on crash. The steering wheel spun at the last second, and their car veered away from the impact. Rory heard the blare of car horns and the sound of shouting voices. He and April were traveling up the middle of the street, forcing oncoming traffic to swerve and brake sharply to avoid them.

Rory stomped down again on the brake, but the car just kept accelerating. Rory clung to the wheel, terrified that at any moment they would crash headlong into some oncoming vehicle and be killed.

"Turn right onto Warren Road," the grating, mechanical voice roared.

The car lurched to the right.

"Warren Road?" April screamed. "Where is that?"

Rory had no breath to reply, but he was beginning to understand what was happening. The evil thing controlling the car had a plan for them.

He tried once again to hold the steering wheel, but it was no good. It blistered his hands and refused to move the way he tried to make it. He felt sick with

158

terror. His mind clouded over, and he slumped back into the seat.

"Warren Road," he finally said. "It's the road where the bridge is missing."

The two passengers stared blankly at each other as they approached their destination.

Don't escape yet! Here's a quick bite from "An Apple a Day"—
just one of three terrifying tales to be found in

THE
MIDNIGHT
LIBRARY
—
VOICES

AN APPLE A DAY

Tim Barnett was beginning to wonder if a person could melt if the sun was too hot.

He wiped sweat from his face and glanced up at the cloudless blue sky. The sun had been shining since he'd woken that morning. In fact, it had been shining ever since Tim had arrived at his grandmother's farm three days ago — not that he was complaining. He loved the hot weather, and with another nine days to go before his parents came to pick him up, he hoped the sun would continue to shine as brightly as it was shining now.

Tim biked along the narrow dirt track, stopping

occasionally to peer across the fields that stretched away in all directions. The grass and weeds on either side of the track were almost as high as his waist, and the fields beyond were equally overgrown.

He rounded a slight bend, and the farm and its outbuildings came back into view. As well as the farmhouse itself, there was a barn, a milking shed, some stables, a garage where the tractor had been stored, and a couple of rusted pigpens — long since abandoned. Pieces of old farmyard equipment dotted the main yard and the areas nearby like the rusted skeletons of metallic dinosaurs. All untouched since his grandfather's death.

Over the years, during his many visits to Grandma's, Tim had explored the entire farm. The barn in particular had proved to be full of amazing stuff — old farm tools like huge scythes and rusted sickles were propped up everywhere like the abandoned weapons of some strange army. Tim liked the stillness in there and, when the weather got unbearably hot, it was pleasant and cool inside, with its high roof and long, splintered shadows.

The barn was also home to one of the largest spiders he'd ever seen in his life. It mostly dwelled high up in the eaves of the barn, but Tim could still make out its eight-legged shape whenever it ventured forth to feast on its latest victim. Its massive webs were all over the barn. Tim had found the remains of flies, wasps, and even other spiders in its silken traps. It was as if the spider was making the barn its own.

Grandpa had died seven years earlier, when Tim was just four; he had only a few memories of him. Dad had tried to persuade Grandma to come and live with them at their home in Boston but she'd said the farm had always been her home and she didn't intend to leave it. Well, what she'd actually said was, "There's a place for everything and everything in its place."

And later, when Tim's dad had tried to tell Grandma that she might not be able to look after the place on her own, she'd smiled, saying, "Don't judge a book by its cover."

That was another one of her sayings. Grandma had a saying for anything and everything and, if he was honest, Tim sometimes found them really irritating.

If he was up a little later than usual in the morning it was, "Early to bed, early to rise, makes you healthy, wealthy, and wise."

If he ate too quickly, he was ". . . eating as if your belly thinks your throat's been cut."

Grandma was superstitious, too. Not just about things like not walking under ladders — Tim knew all about that — but also about strange things he'd never heard of.

One night while they were eating their dinner, he'd reached across the table for the mashed potatoes and knocked over the salt shaker. Right away, Grandma had told him to throw a pinch of salt over his left shoulder.

"Why, Grandma?" he'd asked her, laughing.

"To blind the devil sitting on your shoulder," she'd told him sternly, making sure he completed the strange ritual.

Tim had done as she'd told him, even though it all seemed a little weird at the time, to say the least.

He was startled from his thoughts by a large black crow taking off from a nearby tree. Watching as the bird rose into the cloudless sky, Tim continued biking along one of the many overgrown paths that criss-crossed the farmland like thick brown veins. He had discovered dozens of them during his visits, but he wondered how many more still lay hidden.

Approaching the farmhouse, Tim aimed for a dusty-looking patch of ground. He put down one foot and hit the rear brake, skidding dramatically to a halt. Clouds of dust rose into the dry air.

With a broad grin of satisfaction on his face, Tim looked up to see his grandmother standing in the doorway of the farmhouse, clutching a large glass of lemonade.

"Here's something cold to drink," she said, smiling at him through her large, round glasses, the sun reflecting off her snow-white hair.

"Did you see how fast I was going, Grandma?" Tim asked, gratefully receiving the drink from her and taking a huge gulp.

"Yes, I did. Be careful. You don't want to fall off."

Tim rolled his eyes. "Don't worry, Grandma. Wait until you see what I've got planned for tomorrow," he went on excitedly.

Grandma looked up at the cloudless sky. "Touch wood, the weather stays nice for you," she said.

Tim rolled his eyes again. If he had a dollar for every time he'd heard her say "touch wood" when she was wishing for something, he could afford to buy that new skateboard he wanted.

That evening, the two of them sat watching television together. Banjo, Grandma's beagle, lay on the rug by the old, open fireplace. Tim munched noisily on an apple from the fruit bowl on the coffee table.

"Watch out for the seeds," she told him, chuckling. "You don't want a tree growing in your tummy!"

Tim laughed and took another bite. *Grandma and her crazy sayings*, he thought.

There was a program on about farming in the old days, and how it used to be a big business. Tim watched with interest as the brown-and-white photos and film clips flashed across the screen one after another. "Hey — that's exactly like the one in Grandpa's barn!" he said, pointing at an old plow on the screen.

"You're right," Grandma replied. "Your grandfather used that plow for more than thirty years. Even when new ones came along, he stuck with it. He said that just because it was old, it didn't mean that it was useless."

Suddenly, Grandma turned to Tim and held his hand tightly. "I still miss your grandfather, you know. But God moves in mysterious ways." She relaxed her grip and searched for a tissue to dry her teary eyes. "He must have thought it was your grandfather's time."

Tim gave his grandmother a comforting hug, and then turned back to the TV. But now all he could think about was how little he knew about his grandfather's death. He had been told that Grandpa had been killed in an accident on the farm. No one had ever spoken to him about the actual *details* of how Grandpa had died, but then again, Tim reasoned, he had never really asked. Once, quite a long time ago, Tim had heard his mom and dad talking about it, when they thought that he was asleep. Dad had said that the accident had been unusual. Strange. And all Grandma had said when Tim had asked her about it was, "There are some things you're better off not knowing."

To discover Tim's fate, read
The Midnight Library, Volume I: Voices.

YOUR FEARS WILL FIND YOU.

3 TERRIFYING TALES FROM

THE MIDNIGHT LIBRARY

I CAN SEE YOU

DAMIEN GRAVES

SCHOLASTIC

Michael thinks there's no harm in playing outside after dark.
He's gravely mistaken.

Jake and Brandon are identical twins.
They might be identically doomed.

Carrie receives a free gift when she purchases a magazine.
She's about to have serious issues.

SCHOLASTIC

www.scholastic.com

M